AN EYE FOR AN EYE

A WATER WITCH COZY MYSTERY - BOOK THREE

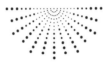

SAM SHORT

WWW.SAMSHORTAUTHOR.COM

ISBN: 9781549505492

❀ Created with Vellum

For Mum and Alan. Thank you for everything - I love you both more than words could ever say.

Book One - Under Lock and Key

Book Two - Four and Twenty Blackbirds

CHAPTER ONE

osie purred and curled into a tight ball on my lap as Mabel the goose gave a low growl and lifted her head in response to an owl's hoot which echoed over the water outside.

"You don't own the canal," laughed Willow, placing a hand on the goose's back. "There's plenty of room for other animals here too. Quieten down."

I studied the goose. Or dog — depending on how you perceived the situation. The white bird had been made to think she was a dog when my grandmother had accidentally cast a spell on her. My sister and I had become accustomed to welcoming the goose aboard the boat we lived on together, for affection or scraps of food. It would be odd to see her acting like a normal goose again if Granny decided to take the potion she'd been gifted by another witch. The potion would cure her rather serious case of witch dementia and reverse any disastrous spells she'd cast while her magic had been affected. Mabel the goose was a lovely creature, but I supposed she'd be happier when she was a normal bird again and not some sort of hybrid creature with a beak and wings who cocked her leg when she went to the toilet.

Granny would be returning to Wickford in the morning, along with Boris the enchanted goat. They'd been on holiday together in Wales for a week, and I dreaded to think how an elderly witch and a sixty-something year old Chinese acupuncturist — trapped in the body of a goat by another of Granny's errant spells — could possibly have lived together peacefully in a caravan for seven days. As Willow had pointed out though — we'd seen nothing on the TV news or read anything in the newspapers, so if Granny and Boris *had* drawn any attention to themselves, at least they'd managed to keep themselves away from any media attention.

Willow stood up and made her way through the narrow canal boat. "Hot chocolate?" she offered, standing in the galley kitchen. "It'll help us sleep. I don't know about you, but I can't wait for tomorrow. I'm as excited as I used to be when Mum took us on holiday when we were little!"

I smiled. The trip was hardly going to be a holiday, but I understood what she meant. Tomorrow was going to be a big day. Maeve — the powerful witch who'd conjured up the magical dimension known as The Haven, had asked for the help of my policeman boyfriend, Barney. It was unprecedented that a mortal person be allowed to cross from our world into The Haven, but Maeve had said the problem she needed help with could not be solved by magic. She needed the help of an old fashioned mortal policeman. "I am excited," I admitted. "Even more so since I found out Mum's arranged with Maeve that we can take the boat into The Haven. *The Water Witch* has been moored up for too long, she deserves a nice cruise."

Willow nodded her agreement and repeated her offer of hot chocolate, a carton of milk in one hand and her other hand on a shapely hip.

I nodded. "Make mine very milky, please," I said as my sister lit the gas stove and began heating milk in a small pan. She added chocolate powder to the milk and the boat filled with the complimentary aromas of burning gas and warm chocolate. I sighed and stroked Rosie. Living on a canal narrowboat with my sister was awesome at the best of times — but when it was dark outside and we sat next to one another on the small sofa drinking late-night hot chocolate — life was as near to perfect as I could imagine. It would have been nice to have Barney next to me too, but inviting Barney to stay on the boat overnight wouldn't have been fair to my sister.

Willow had only moved aboard a few weeks ago — before Barney and I were *an item*. Giving Willow the space and privacy I'd promised her when I'd invited her to move aboard with me was the right thing to do. Anyway, she'd have to get used to a crowded boat for the foreseeable future. Barney, Mum, Granny and Boris were all joining us the following day as we took the boat into The Haven. I hadn't worked out *exactly* where everyone would sleep, but I'd already resigned myself to the fact that my bed would be handed over to Granny. She might have acted like she was still in her teens, but she was way past the age I'd expect anyone to sleep on furniture which folded down into a makeshift bed.

Willow carefully poured the drinking chocolate into two mugs and passed me one as she sat down. She pointed at the pair of wooden clogs on the dinette table. "They don't look very powerful, do they?" she said.

The clogs were a magical artefact that allowed anybody to enter The Haven — even a mortal with no magical powers, but Willow was right — they didn't look very impressive.

I laughed. "No, but then again, Granny doesn't look very powerful either, but she's managed to cause havoc throughout her lifetime!"

Willow snorted as she laughed, and squealed as

the hot liquid in her mouth dribbled down her chin. "Ow! I burnt my lip!"

I clicked my fingers and cast a minor healing spell.

"Wow," said Willow, touching her lip and sounding as impressed as I felt. "You're turning into a magical dynamo! You stopped the burning."

I'd been studying the big spell book that Granny had given Willow and me, but even I was impressed at how much I'd learnt in such a short time. I wasn't big-headed though, and certainly didn't think of myself as a dynamo of any type — let alone a magical one. "That spell's pretty easy to be honest," I lied. "You could learn to cast it in no time at all."

It hadn't been easy to learn. As Granny had told me — spells which change the physical biology of a human being or animal were the hardest to master. I'd had a few mishaps attempting to learn the healing spell, including growing an extra toe which had throbbed with as much pain as the toe I'd stubbed and was attempting to heal. I didn't tell her, but the spell which I'd just cast on my sister was my first successful attempt at a healing spell.

Willow drained the last of her drinking chocolate and stretched her arms towards the low ceiling. "I'm ready for bed," she said through a yawn.

I was tired too and I was certain that the next day would demand I was well rested. "Me too," I acknowledged. "I'll let you use the bathroom first, you look even more tired than I feel."

When we'd both cleaned our teeth, and Willow had applied the moisturiser she insisted on using every night — even though her skin had always been smoother than a Frenchman's chat up lines — we went to our bedrooms at opposite ends of the boat. I opened the doors that led from my room to the bow decking and knew that Willow would be opening the doors that led from her room onto the stern decking. It was a warm night, and there's something truly beautiful about falling asleep with a breeze on your face and listening to the splashes and calls of the nocturnal canal wildlife. Sleep came quickly, and I dreamed of navigating *The Water Witch* along the rivers of The Haven as we made our way to The City of Shadows and whatever mystery Maeve required help in solving.

Being woken by a tall ginger haired man, grinning inanely, and wearing a policeman's uniform, is not everyone's idea of the perfect start to the day, but as Barney gave me a kiss and handed me a steaming mug of black coffee, I was as content as I'd ever been.

"Breakfast's on," said Barney, quite unnecessarily

— my nose was already twitching as the salty aroma of frying bacon reached my bedroom. "Willow's gone to the shop to make sure it's locked and secure, and your grandmother and Boris are waiting for your mother to finish cooking breakfast. We're all set to go!"

I looked Barney up and down. "Why the uniform? We're going to The Haven, you can wear whatever clothes you like — you're not on official Wickford police business."

"Gladys said it would be best if I arrived in uniform," said Barney. "She thinks it will give me some credentials and authority. I've packed a suitcase full of other clothes too — don't worry."

Granny had a valid point. If Barney was to gain the trust of the magical community in The Haven, and have them accept him as a figure of authority, it was best that he at least looked the part. I sipped my coffee and squeezed his hand. "And you look so handsome in your uniform too, so there is that added bonus," I said.

Barney raised an eyebrow. "You've always said my trousers were too short."

I laughed. He was right. I had said that — and meant it, but Barney was so tall that the police uniform department didn't stock a pair of trousers which fitted him correctly. It was hard to get any clothes that fitted him well. As well as being extremely tall, Barney was thin for his height. Not *too* thin, but a few extra pounds around his waist and a few inches of additional width across his shoulders would have allowed clothes to fit him, rather than hang off him. I smiled at him. "You look extremely handsome in your uniform," I said. "Now go and sit with the others while I get dressed. I won't be long."

I listened to Barney laughing with my family as I got dressed, and joined them on the shore just as Mum brought out plates of food and a large teapot adorned with a colourful knitted tea-cosy. The teapot was from the boat's kitchen, but I'd never seen the cosy before. I knew that when Mum packed to go away, she liked to pack as many home comforts as she could fit in her suitcase. I guessed that somewhere amongst her luggage would be a Lionel Richie CD and possibly even a full set of silver cutlery.

I hugged Granny and tickled Boris behind one of his horns as I took a seat at the picnic table next to Barney. Boris grunted a *good morning* and Granny reached across the table and squeezed my hand in hers. "Hi, sweetheart," she said. "It's lovely to see you. Ignore Boris's grunting. He's in a foul mood today."

"What's wrong with you, Boris?" I asked. "It's not like you to be in a bad mood."

The goat looked up at me. "Let's just say that your grandmother has a heavy foot, Penelope. She sped all the way home from Wales, and it was through good luck and *not* through any skill on her behalf that we didn't die in a fiery car wreck. I'm still trembling inside, Penelope — it will be nice to spend a few days cruising slowly along rivers in your boat."

Granny smiled. "You bought me a powerful Range Rover, Boris. If you think I'm going to potter about in it you've got another thing coming. I intend to make that bitch burn rubber!"

Barney cleared his throat. "It's probably not a good idea to admit to a speeding offence while you're in my company, Gladys. I am an officer of the law after all."

Granny fixed Barney with a stare that made the policeman gulp. "I dare you, Barney Dobkins! I double dare you to even suggest that you'll do so much as tell me what the speed limit on the motorway is. Go on, Barney... I'll bloody —"

"That's enough!" barked Mum. "We'll have no language like that at the breakfast table. We're all about to take a trip together on a small boat, so I suggest we learn to be polite to one another!" She turned her attention to Barney, and frowned. "But seriously, Barney. No one likes a grass. What were you thinking?"

Barney nodded and dropped his gaze. "It was habit," he said. "But it's hard to listen to people telling me they've committed crimes, especially

SAM SHORT

crimes which could hurt somebody else." He looked at Granny. "Try and keep the speed down okay? I don't want to be called out to a car wreck one day and find you at the wheel. That's all."

Granny raised an eyebrow and sipped her tea, but said nothing.

Willow chose the opportune moment to emerge at the bottom of the path which led to the magic shop we ran together. She broke the silence with a shout and gave us a cheery wave. "Save some bacon for me, I'm hungrier than ten men on a diet!" she demanded.

Mum spoke under her breath. "How she keeps that figure is a mystery to me," she said. "She eats more than I did at her age and I had a heck of a job keeping the pounds off."

Granny gave a laugh which echoed across the canal and startled a moorhen. It flapped its way through a vibrant raft of lily-pads and sought refuge in the slender reeds which covered the opposite bank. "You were a little fatty from the day you could *say* food, Maggie! It's no mystery that you couldn't keep the pounds off. The only mystery is how I managed to find clothes to fit you!" she said.

Barney gulped.

Boris snorted.

Granny laughed again, and Mum shook her head. "Your parenting skills are second to none, Mother," she said, buttering herself two thick slices of bread and sandwiching four crispy bacon rashers between them. "But you do make a good point. I *have* always enjoyed my food."

Willow took a seat at the table and helped herself to breakfast. She watched mum bite into the sandwich and lick her lips. "Mum!" she said. "You're eating outside and there are insects everywhere!"

Mum smiled. "You can thank Boris for that," she said, speaking as she chewed. "He worked really hard to get me to where I am today. He's a fine psychologist, and an even finer friend."

The man trapped inside Boris the goat's body was an Oxford educated gentleman who had done many things in his life, including almost finishing a psychology course. He'd offered to help mum overcome her fear of eating outside when insects were present, and as mum took another bite of her sandwich and waved a fat dragonfly from her face, it seemed that he'd accomplished what he'd set out to do.

"I was happy to help," said Boris, "phobias can be awful to live with, but are often surprisingly easy to cure. Yours was a simple case, Maggie." He looked at *The Water Witch.* "Are we leaving soon?" he said, "I'm considerably excited about visiting The Haven. It sounds so perfectly wonderful, and maybe I'll find out more about who I am whilst I'm there."

Boris, or Charleston to be precise, had recently

found out that he came from a family of witches — a secret which had been hidden from him by his family. We weren't sure if he possessed the gift of magic, and we wouldn't know until Granny had cured her dementia and put Charleston's mind back into his own body, but a trip to the haven might be beneficial nonetheless.

I wiped my greasy hands on a paper towel. "We'll leave soon," I said. "Uncle Brian and Susie will be on the bridge at half past nine. They'll wave us forward when there are no people or cars nearby. Then I'll open the portal and the bridge will become our way into The Haven!"

"Brian should be on the boat with us," said Granny. "Not on look out duty. He's far more important than that."

"Brian wanted to stay," said Mum. "He's focusing on opening his *business*, remember?"

Granny narrowed her eyes and her purple glasses threatened to slide from the bridge of her nose. "Did you put sarcastic emphasis on the word *business*, my dear? Because if you did, I'll enjoy hearing why, you jealous upstart."

Mum sighed. "My brother is pretending to be a hypnotherapist and using magic to help people break their bad habits. It's a very dubious *business* model if you ask me." Mum looked at Barney. "What do you think, Police Constable Dobkins? Surely it's illegal too? Gaining money by misrepresentation, or something like that?"

Barney blushed for the first time that day. Barney had a problem with blushing, but even I'd have blushed — or withered — under the gaze which Granny had fixed him with "Well?" she said. "Is what my first born is doing illegal, young man?"

Barney slumped in his seat. "I don't know! Probably, but there are no laws regarding magic in the British legal system. We used to have laws a long time ago, but the outcome was always miserable for the witches involved. It usually ended up in a drowning or a burning at the stake."

"Are you threatening to burn Brian at the stake?" shouted Granny, getting to her feet and holding a hand before her with sparks dancing at the fingertips. "Cos' I'll burn you first, you ginger muppet!"

"Calm down, Gladys," said Boris placing his front hooves on the table. "You're suffering from witch dementia! You shouldn't even be threatening to cast a spell — anything could happen! Now put your hand away and sit down! Barney wasn't threatening Brian, and you know it. Anyway, you like Barney. You told me he would make a fine grandson-in-law."

Granny smiled. "Yes, I did, didn't I?" she looked around the table with pride replacing the expression of anger. "It was a pun! Do you all get it? He'll be my grandson-in-law if he makes an honest woman of

Penny, and he's a dirty fed, hence the *law* part of the pun!"

"Very good," said Willow. "Very clever, Granny."

"Funny," I acknowledged. "Don't anyone arrange a visit to a hat shop just yet though. Barney and I have only been together for a few weeks."

Barney cleared his throat. "I'm not a dirty fed, Gladys. I'm a police officer, and anyway the term *fed* is American."

"I didn't want to call you a pig, Barney. Not in the presence of bacon and sausages anyway. It seemed disrespectful," said Granny. "So I went yank on your ass."

"Why do our conversations always end up so far away from where they started?" asked Mum. "Let's focus on the task in hand for once. Is everybody ready to go? Is all the luggage on the boat, and is the boat prepared?"

The last question was aimed at me. "The boat's ready," I confirmed. "*The Water Witch* has a full fuel tank, fresh gas canisters, a full water tank and a greased stern gland. She's ready to go when everybody else is."

Willow looked at her watch. "It's nine o'clock," she said. "Uncle Brian and Susie will be making their way to the bridge. We'd better get going."

"Any more questions before we leave?" asked Mum. "Just remember — the most important thing is that everybody is touching the clogs when we pass through the portal, apart from Penelope of course, as it's going to be her portal we're passing through. The magic clogs will ensure we all get through safely as long as we're touching at least one of them, okay?"

Everyone nodded, and Barney cleared his throat. "I have a question," he said.

"Yes?" said Mum.

"How does it work? The portal I mean. I've seen Penny going through hers, and it looks a little scary. I'm the only one among all of us who doesn't have magic. Will I be safe? I don't understand what a portal is."

"I don't have magic," said Boris. "As far as I know at this juncture in time anyway."

"You come from a family of witches though, Boris," I said. "I'm sure that when Granny takes the cure for her dementia, and you find yourself back in your body, you'll have magic. I know it."

"When will you take the cure, Granny?" said Willow. "Maeve gave it to you almost two weeks ago."

Boris looked away and Granny fiddled with her necklace. "I don't want to talk about it right now, thank you. I'll take it in my own good time." She pointed a finger at the breast pocket of Barney's jacket. "Pass me a piece of paper from your police notebook, and your pencil, and I'll show you how a portal works and put your mind at rest, Barney."

I handed Granny a white paper towel. "Use this. Barney can't remove pages from his police notebook, Granny. He could be accused of destroying evidence. Even I know that."

Granny sighed and took the pencil from Barney as she smoothed out the paper towel on the table. "He's wearing his uniform to a magical dimension, Penelope. I'm sure the police authorities would have a bigger problem with that than with a missing page from a notebook."

"Just show him what you want him to see, Mother," said Mum. "We must get going."

"Do you look at the stars, Barney?" said Granny, using her finger to test the sharpness of the pencil point.

"Of course," said Barney. "I like stargazing."

Granny smiled. "Those stars are not there anymore, Barney, but they're so far away that the light from the explosions which destroyed them is still reaching us, millions of years later. That's all a lot of the stars are, Barney — the light from an explosion long ago."

"I know," said Barney. "It's amazing."

Granny nodded. "Space is vast, Barney. It's why a lot of people argue against the existence of aliens who have the technology to visit our planet — space is just too huge. It would take them millions of years to cross the void."

"I've read about that," said Barney.

Granny licked her lips. "What if they didn't need to cross that distance though, Barney? Maybe they could get here quickly if the distance wasn't so great?"

"That make sense," said Barney.

Granny folded the paper towel in two and held it up for us all to see. "Imagine The Haven is a long way away, Barney."

Barney nodded. "Okay."

Granny held the pencil near the paper. "Imagine this pencil is the boat we're going to be traveling through the portal on, Barney."

Barney nodded again.

Granny struck the folded paper viciously with the pencil point and held the impaled paper aloft. "Boom!" she said. "That's how it works."

"Huh?" said Barney.

"How does it work, Granny?" said Willow. "What does the paper represent?"

"Well, I don't know. Willow," snapped Granny. "That's what the scientists do in films when they need to explain cross dimensional travel, and nobody questions them!"

"It's because they offer an explanation too, Granny," said Willow. "They don't just poke a hole in some paper and expect people to understand what they're talking about."

"It's because they're men! Isn't it?" spat Granny, throwing the pencil and paper at Barney. "Curse the patriarchy! Curse the scientists in films, and curse space travel! I've had enough of the lot of them!"

Mum put her hand on Barney's shoulder. "Relax, Barney," she said. "Traveling through Penny's portal is new to all of us, you're not the only one who's trying something new."

Mum was right. She could have opened her own portal to travel through if she'd wanted, but Granny couldn't open hers while suffering from witch dementia and Willow and Boris had no way of opening their own portals — Willow was yet to earn her Haven entry spell, and Boris was a goat. Trusting the magic clogs would be a leap of faith for everybody on the boat apart from me.

My phone beeped. "It's a message from Susie," I said, defusing the tension. "Her and Uncle Brian are at the bridge. They're waiting for us, we should get aboard the boat. Next stop — The Haven."

CHAPTER TWO

The engine vibrated beneath my feet as I gave *The Water Witch* a burst of power and guided her around the final bend in the canal as the bridge appeared in the distance. Barney stood to the right of me at the steering tiller, and Granny and Mum sat below deck at the dinette table, with the magical clogs in front of them.

Boris peered up at me through the open doors of my bedroom and gave as close to a smile as a goat could manage. The goat's teeth had been yellow and grass worn when the animal had existed purely as a goat, but had become further discoloured since Charleston Huang had inhabited Boris's body and continued to satisfy his penchant for brandy and cigars. Even Boris's coarse white hair carried the aroma of cigar smoke, which I had to admit, was more agreeable than the odour the goat had emitted when it had been tied to a stake in Granny's back garden.

With the sun in my eyes it was hard to make out the shapes of anyone standing on the bridge, but as the trees on the bank thickened their uppermost branches into a canopy which stretched across the narrow canal, it became easy to make out the spherical figure of Uncle Brian. Susie stood next to him, dwarfed by my uncle's bulk, waving a hand in the air. "It's all clear!" she shouted. "No cars or people in sight, and Brian has cast a spell which will keep people away! It's safe to open a portal!"

I waved my acknowledgment, and sent Barney below deck. "You'd better go and take hold of a clog," I said. "And when we go through the portal make sure to keep your eyes open, it becomes very disorientating otherwise."

I'd learnt from my first trip through a portal that closing your eyes when passing from one dimension to another confused the brain and brought on a dizzying case of vertigo.

Barney kissed my cheek. "I'll see you on the other side," he said, rather ominously, as he descended the three steps into my bedroom where Boris waited.

"Be sure to put a hoof into a clog, Boris," I said, reminding him of our plan. "And make sure Rosie's paw is touching them too."

We'd been sure to leave Mabel the goose safe at my mooring in Wickford, but I wouldn't go anywhere without Rosie on board. She'd been my constant and loyal traveling companion ever since I'd bought my boat.

Boris grunted. "Don't worry about us, just concentrate on steering the boat in a straight line."

He made a valid point. My boat was seven feet wide, and the space below the bridge was just a couple of inches wider. It could be tricky to navigate a narrowboat beneath one of the smaller canal bridges on the best of days, without the addition of a magical portal masking the route. "Don't worry," I said, "I'll get us through safely. You have my word."

"Have you seen that in a vision, Penny?" asked Boris. "Or is it just a guess to make us feel safer?"

I'd recently found out that I possessed the gift of seeing, and my first vision had helped solve a murder. I'd had no more visions since then, and had been told by my mother that I may not have another for years to come. I laughed. "No vision I'm afraid, Boris," I said. "You'll just have to take my word for it and put your trust in me."

Barney smiled. "We trust you, Penny."

Barney and Boris disappeared as they made their way through the boat to the dinette table, and Mum shouted to confirm that everybody was in position. "We're all set, Penny!" she said.

The bridge neared and I prepared to cast my haven entry spell. Susie leaned out over wall of the bridge and smiled. "I'll keep an eye on your shop!" she said. "I really wish I was coming with you!"

Susie lived in a flat directly above *The Spell Weavers* — the magic shop which Willow and I ran. She'd been unable to take the time away from her job as a journalist to join us on our trip into the haven, but had been consoled when I'd pointed out that now we possessed the magic clogs which allowed mortals safe passage into The Haven, she'd be able to join us on a future trip. "Thank you, Susie!" I shouted.

"Have a fabulous time!" yelled Uncle Brian, looking as dapper as he always did, in a bright red jacket which I knew would be fashioned from crushed velvet. "And don't do anything I wouldn't do!"

I gave him a smile and a wave. Uncle Brian had only recently moved to Wickford from London, but was a welcome addition to the Weaver family. "We'll have a great time," I assured him, my fingertips crackling with magic as I prepared to cast my spell.

The bow of the boat, sixty feet to my front, neared the bridge, and I concentrated hard. Portals were normally opened in doorways, but Maeve had promised my mother that a portal could be opened in anything which was considered an entrance. I tasted the familiar metallic copper flavour in my mouth which accompanied any spell I cast, and forced the build-up of magic from my fingertips.

The water beneath the bridge churned and a warm breeze blew from the space between the cold damp walls of the archway. A soft gold light hovered in the entrance, and spread slowly until it filled the space below the bridge. "It worked!" I shouted.

"Good luck!" yelled Susie, as the bow of the boat slid into the light.

I concentrated on keeping the steering tiller in position as I nudged the power leaver forward a fraction, giving The Water Witch the extra power she'd need to remain on a straight course. The breeze grew stronger and my long dark hair lifted from my shoulders. I shielded my eyes from the leaves which the wind blew from the trees, and shouted a final farewell to the two people on the bridge as *The Water Witch* was completely enveloped by the shimmering wall of gold.

———

WIND and bright light made it hard to keep the boat's course straight, but almost as soon as I'd entered the portal, I was steering the boat along an unfamiliar but beautiful stretch of water. "Is everyone okay down there?" I shouted, slowing the boat and guiding the bow towards the bank-side.

SAM SHORT

"We're just dandy!" shouted Boris. "Are we there yet?"

"Yes!" I shouted, "come on up."

The bow of the boat nudged the bank and I leapt ashore with two iron mooring hoops which slid easily into the soft earth. I hammered them home with the mallet Willow tossed ashore, and tied off the bow and stern ropes.

"It's beautiful here" said Barney stepping ashore and offering Granny a steadying hand as she climbed from the boat. "It's *really* beautiful."

He was right. The stretch of water we were on was wider than the narrow canals I was used to navigating at home, reminding me of the River Thames in its middle course. The banks were alive with lush foliage and fragrant wildflowers, and a fat trout leapt for a fly which hovered suicidally close to the surface of the pristine water. Swallows dipped and dived as they caught insects on the wing, and a frog croaked from its hidden position in a clump of bull rushes.

On my first trip to The Haven I'd noted how clean and alive with life the magical dimension was, putting me in mind of the paintings I'd seen of England in the days before pollution had poisoned the landscape and waterways. It truly was a beautiful place, and a peaceful serenity washed over me as I imagined journeying along the river. I closed my eyes and took a deep breath of the sweet-smelling air, enjoying the sun on my face and the sound of birds and insects.

"Why does the sky seem a little red?" said Boris, leaping gracefully from *The Water Witch* and gazing at the scenery.

The peachy tint to the sky was strongest where the snowy peaks of distant mountains touched the sky, but the whole vast sky had a slight reddish hue to it. I'd noticed it when I was last in The Haven, but there had been far more important things to concentrate on than the colour of the sky.

Mum joined us on the shore and scooped her long dark hair behind her head, gathering it into a ponytail which she tied with a bobble she took from her pocket. "The sky is red," she said, "because as Maeve was being burned alive at the stake — she closed her eyes and prepared to die. The red of the sky is the colour of the flames which she could see through her eyelids. It's said that the pain she experienced as the flames began burning her is what caused all her magic to explode form her in a fraction of a second — creating The Haven and transporting her to safety. She's lucky to be alive, but what she created when she thought she was going to die, not only saved her life, but the lives of countless other persecuted witches who fled to The Haven after her. It's quite a story, and we should feel very honoured to be standing here."

Granny gave a low snigger. "It's okay here, but

it's certainly no Oz. Now *that's* a place which would impress me. If I was to conjure up a magical land I'd fashion it after Oz, populating it with a mixture of folk, but I'd most certainly throw in a few short fellows who'd dance, sing, and jump at my every command. It does the soul good to look down on others every now and again — both figuratively and literally. No flying monkeys though, those buggers would cause havoc with a banana plantation, and I'd be sure to plant a few of those. And a pear orchard. I like pears. I like Oz."

Boris lifted his nose from the flower he was smelling. "Is that how you see me, Gladys? As somebody you can look down on?"

Granny placed a hand on the goat's back. "You know that's not how I feel about you, Boris. I treat you with the respect and dignity you deserve."

Boris stamped a hoof and snorted. "Then why didn't you take the dementia cure when I asked you to?"

Granny bristled. "This is not the time or place for this conversation, Boris. We're in the company of others."

Mum frowned and gave Granny a stern stare, but just as she was about to speak, the air around us crackled and fizzed. Boris took a few stumbling steps backward and Barney jumped. Two billowing clouds of red smoke swirled into existence in front of us, and in a fraction of a second, with a loud popping sound, there were two extra people in our group.

Maeve and Derek stood side by side, up to their knees in grass, the smoke dispersing around them. Derek carried the staff he'd used to cast a spell over a field full of people the last time we'd seen him, and Maeve gave us a wide friendly smile. "Thank you all for coming," she said. She turned her attention to Barney. "Especially you, lawman. Our need is dire, and you are the only person equipped with the skills to solve a mystery which no amount of magic can help us with."

"Skills," muttered Granny. "I've seen more skills in a circus monkey."

Derek slammed his staff into the river-bank. "Silence, Gladys Weaver. Show some respect to the creator of The Haven!"

Granny narrowed her eyes. "I respect Maeve," she said, "but I find it hard to respect a man who until very recently called himself The Copper Haired Wizard of The West." She turned her back on Maeve and Derek and clambered aboard *The Water Witch*. "Would you be so kind as to accompany me, Boris?" she said. "We should talk."

Boris gave Maeve what was an attempt at an apologetic grin, but was a grimace of yellowed teeth. "Please excuse me, your honour," he said.

Maeve tilted her and gave a gentle laugh, her long

blond hair shining in the sunlight. "Call me Maeve, please. We don't stand on formalities here."

Boris bent his front legs and lowered his chest to the ground in a bow, and Willow hid a giggle behind her hand. The white goat leapt aboard the boat and followed Granny below deck, grumbling to himself as his hind quarters disappeared.

"Gladys Weaver is a rude woman," said Derek. "I don't know why you invited her here, Maeve. It was a blessing when she was struck with dementia and couldn't open her own entry portal. Things have been… peaceful around here without her. If I had my way she'd still be banished from The Haven."

"Well you don't have it your way, Derek!" snapped Maeve. "Every witch is special in my eyes and Gladys is no exception. You'll have to put the past behind you and make your peace with her."

Derek and Gladys had butted heads in the past when Derek, during his time as The Copper Haired Wizard of The West, had cast a community of Haitian Voodoo witches from his lands and conjured a wall of magic to keep them out. Granny had not liked the injustice and had formed a group of witches known as the SJW's — or Social Justice Witches — eventually forcing Derek to tear down the wall. Granny's time as a social justice activist had culminated in her being banished from The Haven for a period of time, and it seemed that Derek still held a grudge.

Derek huffed. "Don't you find it odd that she hasn't taken the cure for her dementia yet, Maeve?" he said, twisting his staff into the ground, the jewels set in the carved knob glinting in the sun. "It was very kind of you to give it to her, I'd have thought she'd have used it by now — don't you?"

Maeve closed her eyes for a moment. "It's her choice, Derek, but yes, I happen to agree with you. I was surprised to see the Chinese acupuncturist still trapped in the body of a goat — as soon as Gladys takes the cure he'll be freed, and I'd have thought that would be best for all concerned. Things will happen in their own time, though. We should allow fate to run its course."

"But —"

"Enough, Derek. We can't force our will on people." Maeve looked at each of us in turn. "Rumour has it that Eva has prepared a welcome feast for the hungry travellers, and Derek and I have been invited. How about we all climb aboard that beautiful boat of yours, Penelope? Eva's village is only two miles downstream and I'd love a trip on *The Water Witch*. We can discuss the reason I've asked for your help over a plate of your aunt's fine cooking."

"I'll meet you there," said Derek, straightening his colourful patchwork jacket. "I'll not be getting on that contraption. Why not use magic if you have it?"

Derek vanished in a cloud of smoke, and Maeve

smiled. "I'm sorry about Derek," she said. "He's old fashioned. He doesn't feel I should be asking for the help of a mortal to solve a haven problem." She smiled at Barney. "No offense meant, Lawman Barney. You're a fine mortal indeed."

"None taken," said Barney, offering Maeve his hand. "Let me help you aboard. You'll love the boat."

CHAPTER THREE

On my first visit to The Haven I'd eaten a meal at the table situated amongst the trees in the orchard at the bottom of Aunt Eva's cottage garden. I'd had no idea that beyond the orchard ran a river, and as I steered the boat alongside the bank I found myself looking forward to the day in the distant future on which I'd move to The Haven on a permanent basis. I'd live in a cottage just like Aunt Eva's, and moor my boat at the foot of my garden — ready for the regular trips along the river I imagined myself taking during my immortal existence in the magical dimension.

Maeve had driven the boat for most of the short journey and had laughed with joy as *The Water Witch* had responded to the instructions she gave it through the steering tiller. Her face was tinted with a happy red blush as she climbed ashore and helped Barney tie the boat to the trunks of two trees whose lowest branches dipped their leaves in the water. "That was the most fun I've had in a long time!" she said, tying a firm knot in the rope and moving aside as Boris leapt ashore.

Boris and Granny had spent the journey in Willow's bedroom, at the bow end of the boat, speaking about the issue they so obviously had between them. I didn't ask them what was wrong, neither did Mum, Barney or Willow — we'd been enjoying ourselves far too much to worry about a disagreement between Boris and Granny. Over the last few months, since Charleston had been magicked into the body of Boris the goat, the pair had had at least three disagreements a week. The only thing different about this one was that it seemed more personal. I made a mental note to bring it up with Granny when I had her on my own.

I studied Barney as he gazed around. He was still coming to terms with the fact that he was in a magical dimension, the existence of which he'd only been made aware of two short weeks ago. We'd told him to curb his excitement a little when he came to The Haven, because if he wanted to be taken seriously, he couldn't act like a child on his first trip to a toy shop. He was doing a good job so far, but it was easy to sense his awe. His eyes glinted with excitement and his nose twitched as the aroma of cooking drifted through the trees which hid Aunt Eva's garden from view.

Boris was way ahead of Barney. "I smell Italian food," he said, licking his lips and wetting the hairs which formed his beard. "I'm quite the fan of Italian food." He gave Granny a sideways look. "If it's prepared correctly of course."

Granny's blue rinse perm bounced as she approached Boris at speed. "Was that meant as a dig at me, Boris?" she said, bending at the waist and staring the animal in the eyes. "It had better not be, because I put everything into making that spaghetti bolognese for you. I can't help it if you're a fussy eater!"

Boris took a step backwards. "You used child's spaghetti in tomato sauce, Gladys. From a tin! The type shaped like letters, and you didn't even ensure I had the letters on my plate to spell out *this meal sucks big time*. It was hardly fine Mediterranean dining!"

"We were on holiday. In a caravan," said Granny. "I did what I could, besides — I never got much practice at making fancy nancy dishes — Norman, rest his soul, was a simple man. He liked his meat and two potatoes, and he didn't whine if the gravy had lumps in it! He didn't pester me for posh nosh. He was happy with what he got!"

Maeve clapped, the sound startling a frog from a

lily pad. "Please," she said, "stop that at once. The Haven is a place of peace, most of the time. Save your arguments for later and concentrate on being nice to one another." She took a step along the overgrown pathway which disappeared into the trees. "Come on. If we're not quick, Derek will have eaten all the food before we even get to the table."

We formed a line behind Maeve and followed her along the narrow pathway as the sound of a woman's laughter grew louder.

"That's my sister's flirting giggle," said Granny from behind me. "I may not have seen her for some time, but I can tell from a mile away when she's trying to get her claws into a man. She's in her young body too — that laugh gives it away."

The pathway opened into a clearing and it seemed that Granny's observation had been correct. Sitting at the large wooden table among the fruit trees and wild flowers was Hilda — the elderly seer who had foretold of my power to see the future, Derek — who was chewing on a mouthful of food, and my Aunt Eva — looking more beautiful than I'd ever seen her. When a witch is given their Haven entry spell, they're also afforded the gift of being able to transform themselves between the age they were when they moved from the mortal world for good, and the age they were when they were granted their haven entry spell, *and* any age in between. Aunt Eva had been nineteen when she'd acquired her spell, and she'd chosen to be young today, unlike the last time I'd visited The Haven — when she'd remained in the body of the eighty-nine-year-old she'd been when she chose to make The Haven a permanent home. She looked to be in her early twenties today — a good couple of decades younger than the man she was trying to impress. Though most of Aunt Eva's body was hidden by the table, it was apparent from whom Willow had inherited her shapely figure. Aunt Eva's cleavage burst at the low-cut blouse she wore, and she pressed up close to Derek, filling his plate with offerings from the many dishes and plates which filled the table top.

"Look at that alleyway hussy!" hissed Granny. "All over Derek like he was the last man alive. It's disgusting!"

Mum pushed passed us, spurred on by the sight of the feast. "Try not to be jealous, Mother. Just because your dementia stops you shifting to a younger body, doesn't mean everyone else has to stay old and wrinkly."

Granny laughed. "At least you're admitting you're wrinkly, dear. It's about time."

"I wasn't talking about myself," snorted Mum. "I'm hardly old, and I'm staying this age out of respect for my daughters. They don't want their mother outshining them in the looks department."

"And the weight department," said Granny. "You

were even tubbier when you were younger. Like a fatted piglet. A cute one, but a wobbly one too."

Mum chose to ignore Granny and took a seat at the table, giving the young Aunt Eva a kiss and smiling at Hilda who adjusted the bejeweled eye-patch she wore. I'd learned on my first meeting with Hilda that the eye-patch was for purely decorative purposes, but I had to admit that it did a good job in giving her the aura of mystery which I imagined was a great aid in her existence as a seer of the future.

Granny sat down and scowled at her sister. "You're looking… nice today, Eva. Ashamed of your real age?"

Eva smiled. "It's lovely to see you too, dear sister. How's the dementia?"

Granny mumbled something and helped herself to a large scoop of lasagne. "It's a good job for you that I can't take on my younger form," she said. "I always was the better looking one."

"Granny," said Willow. "You're sisters. You shouldn't be competing with each other!"

Eva laughed and Derek rolled his eyes, popping an olive in his mouth and pushing Aunt Eva's hand away from his arm. "Enough bickering," he said. "I'm trying to eat."

Boris's hooves scrambled for purchase in the grass as Hilda slammed her fist into the table top and screeched. "Danger!" she warned. "Danger!"

Barney leapt to his feet and drew his nightstick, brandishing the weapon above his head. "Where?" he said, twisting his head left and right.

"Calm down everybody," said Maeve, her voice as soft as butter. "Hilda's had a vision." She looked at the old woman. "Is that right, Hilda?"

Hilda nodded. "I see danger greeting you on your journey," she half whispered, looking at each of us in turn.

I grabbed Barney's wrist. "Sit down," I said as he put his nightstick away. "It's okay."

Hilda closed her one visible eye and sighed. "I see romance blossoming too. I see pure love on the horizon."

Barney took my hand and squeezed it, making me blush.

Maeve picked up on my unease and ushered the seer on. "The danger you spoke of is more relevant, Hilda. Tell us more," she said.

Derek grunted. "Are we really going to listen to the ramblings of Hilda?" he said. "If we took everything Hilda said seriously we'd all be hiding under our beds."

"Yes, we are, Derek," snapped Maeve. "Show some respect."

Hilda continued, slowly swaying her torso from side to side as she spoke. "I see danger and love, and I see a man with coal black hair. Beware of him, for he means ill-will to all." She paused for a moment and took a deep breath. "I see great power too, power greater than Maeve's. The power is so great that the person who wields it will rule The Haven if they so choose."

Derek leaned forward in his seat. "Tell us more, Hilda."

"You've changed your tune," said Granny.

"I've heard of this power before," explained Derek. "In an ancient prophecy. If the power Hilda speaks of threatens Maeve's control over The Haven, then it's prudent that we listen."

"I see no more," said Hilda with a shake of her head. "Though you must heed my words."

"Duly noted," said Derek, pushing his plate way from him and taking a small metal tin from his breast pocket. He prised it open and withdrew a small twig which he placed between his teeth and began to chew.

Boris raised his head from the plate of cold meats and salad he was eating. "Liquorice root?" he said, sniffing the air. "Would you be so kind as to allow me one, Derek? I've not had one in years, and I find they cleanse the palate rather well."

Derek raised an eyebrow and took another twig from the tin, tossing it into the grass in front of Boris. "Be my guest," he said, as the goat gripped the stick in his mouth and settled down in the wild flowers to chew. Derek held the tin out. "Anybody else?" he said.

He put the tin away when nobody else took him up on his offer, and watched Barney with amusement as the policeman took his notebook and pencil out and cleared his throat.

"I feel it's my duty to ask some questions," he said, with a nervous strain in his voice. "After all, I was asked to come here to help solve a mystery, but so far, I've been given no indication as to what that mystery is, and we've just been told by a fortune teller that there's danger waiting for us."

Hilda gasped. "I'm no fortune teller, fire haired man of the law. I'm a seer! I require no recompense for my visions. A fortune teller would demand you cross her palm with silver before telling you of your fate, but I do it from the goodness of my heart. I've never been so offended."

"He meant no offence, Hilda," said Maeve, gently. "But Barney is right — it's about time I told everyone why I've asked for their help."

Maeve's forehead creased and everybody quietened down, even Granny, who was informing Aunt Eva that her makeup was sixty-years out of style. The powerful witch took a breath and began speaking. "As you all know." She looked at Barney and Boris. "As *most* of you know, I'm aware of most things that happen in this land. I'm tied to the very essence of the place by invisible strands of energy which keep me informed of happenings." She looked at Granny with an accusatory gleam in her eyes. "That *doesn't* mean I spy on people, despite some folk organising protests in the past which falsely stated the opposite. It means I know if people are in trouble, or if somebody new arrives in The Haven... or, if somebody leaves."

"Yes, we get it," said Granny. "You're the all-seeing eye."

Maeve took Granny's comment in her stride, and chose not to respond. "I should say, I *normally* know when somebody has left The Haven. It's just a feeling I get — one less soul feeding on the magic in the air." Her face darkened. "But recently, some people have been reported missing by their families. You must understand that this sort of thing never happens. People report other people for crimes they've committed, but not for —"

"And for crimes they *haven't* committed," interrupted Granny, her arms crossed and her purple glasses teetering on the tip of her nose.

"You were found guilty of every crime you were ever accused of, Gladys Weaver," scoffed Derek. "*And* some you weren't accused of, but boasted about when you'd had too much wine to keep your mouth shut."

"Enough… please," said Maeve. "People are missing, and they may be in danger."

Barney put the tip of his pencil to paper. "Can you give me some more details please?" he said, his eyes narrowed with concern.

Maeve gave a small nod. "As I said, this is new to us in The Haven. I'm glad to see you're eager to help us, lawman Barney."

"I'm happy to," said Barney.

Maeve continued. "Six witches have vanished off the face of the…" She looked at Derek.

"Radar," he obliged.

"Yes, radar. I try to keep up with the modern parlance of the other world, but it becomes confusing. Anyway, witches began disappearing five months ago, and the sixth one went missing just yesterday. They all resided in The City of Shadows, but aside from that we have no other information. I'm sure they couldn't have left The Haven, as I'd have been aware that they passed through a portal, but neither do I feel like they're *in* The Haven. It's a mystery. There are places in The Haven that my magic can't penetrate for reasons unbeknown to me, but people have searched those areas, and have found no sign of the missing witches." She stared at Barney. "Would your investigative skills be of use to us, lawman?"

"I can do my best," said Barney, "I'd need more information of course."

SAM SHORT

"We have no more information, Lawman. I would suggest you make your way to The City of Shadows and do what you must do to help. We'll pay for your services of course — whether you solve the mystery or not."

Barney put his notebook away and shook his head. "I don't want your payment," he said. "Helping you would be a pleasure."

"We'll discuss it again at a later date," said Maeve. "Meanwhile, let me give you all something to take with you." She handed each of us a small black stone and passed Granny a silver ring to hang from Boris's red collar. "Although I can sense where you'll be while you're in The Haven, I'd like you to carry these. They'll allow me to find you quickly if anything should happen," she said. "They won't work in the parts of The Haven in which my magic can't penetrate, and no magic can be used in those places, but there is only one such area on your route along the river — the Silver Mountains, it should take you half a day to reach them, and then a further half day to reach The City of Shadows."

"Or we could just magic them all there and leave the boat here," said Derek. "That would be my decision."

Maeve sighed. "It's not your decision, Derek. They want to see the sights of The Haven along the

42

way, I'm sure, and it will give them the chance to look out for our missing witches along the route."

Barney stood up. "We should leave right away. Those people could be in trouble."

"I'm ready to go," said Willow, arranging her knife and fork on her empty plate. "I can't wait to see more of The Haven."

I agreed. "We've still got hours of daylight left, we'll travel until dusk and find somewhere to moor up for the night."

Maeve got to her feet. "Although The Haven is a safe place," she said, "be aware of your surroundings. There are dangers here — some I'm aware of and, others I'm yet to experience."

"What sort of dangers?" said Willow.

"When I magicked this land into existence," said Maeve, "everything I knew about the world was recreated here, and you must understand that back in those times, we had a very different understanding of your world."

"She means she believed in dragons," sniggered Granny, "and dwarfs — and I don't mean real dwarfs like Big Jim back in Wickford. He's harmless enough when he's not drunk and angry. I mean dwarfs like the ones in books — the type who live in mines and chop people's heads off for looking at them wrong."

"I'm afraid it's true," said Maeve. "Everything I believed in during my time in the other world, now resides here. Don't be alarmed though. The last dwarf war ended three-hundred years ago, and no dragons have ever been seen — their existence is pure speculation based on my belief system when The Haven was conjured into being."

"Could any of these creatures be responsible for the disappearance of the witches?" said Barney, his voice catching in his throat. "Because I'm a policeman, not a dragon slayer, and I'm far too tall to pick on a dwarf. It wouldn't be fair!"

"It would be oppressive," agreed Granny.

Maeve put a reassuring hand on Barney's arm. "Be calm, lawman. If that were the case I would know. The missing witches have the magic to protect themselves from such creatures, as do the witches you travel with. The answer to the mystery of the missing witches will be found among other witches. Of that I'm sure. Worry not, Barney. The creatures spoken of are rare, and most of them mean no harm anyway. Go now, and travel well. Find my missing witches."

CHAPTER FOUR

*M*aeve, Aunt Eva, and Derek waved us off, with Maeve reminding us that if we needed her help all we needed to do was think about her while holding one of the stones she'd given us. Derek and aunt Eva headed back towards Aunt Eva's garden as soon as the boat was a few metres downstream, but Maeve remained on the bank-side, watching us until we'd rounded a bend in the river.

"Brandy time!" said Boris, as the river widened and the banks thickened with trees. "Gladys, my good lady, would you do the honours please?"

It seemed that Granny and Boris had put their differences aside, and Barney helped Granny onto the flat roof of the boat and lifted Boris up after her. Granny moved a few of the potted plants and herbs aside, and laid a blanket on the sun-warmed roof for the two of them to sit on. With a bottle of brandy between them, and clouds of smoke billowing from the cigar which was clamped safely in the vice which had once been used by my grandfather to tie fishing flies, but had been commandeered by Boris as a smoking aid, the two of them laughed and joked as *The Water Witch* swallowed up the peaceful miles.

"This is nice," said Barney, standing next to me at the steering tiller.

He'd changed out of his police uniform on the sage advice of Maeve. Contrary to what Granny had said, Maeve had explained that it would be better if Barney drew no attention to himself in The Haven. People had an innate nervousness around anybody who represented authority — in our real world, and in The Haven, she'd said. He looked far more suited to a trip along a river on a sunny day while dressed in a t-shirt and shorts anyway. His stab jacket had begun to make him sweat, and his boots had trampled dried soil all over the boat's clean decking. The flip flops which adorned his feet would necessitate a lot less sweeping up after him.

"It is nice," I agreed, raising my voice to compete with the throb of the diesel engine beneath our feet. I took a sip of wine and enjoyed the warm tendrils which spread through my limbs. My homemade elder-berry wine was strong, and I'd never have drunk any while driving my boat in the mortal world, but despite the fact we were on a journey to look for missing witches, we were all in vacation mode. Besides, the river was a lot wider than the canals I was used to navigating, and I was certain that I'd be able to polish off a whole bottle of wine before I turned the boat into a collision risk.

Mum and Willow were below deck, finalising the sleeping arrangements, and their raised voices could be heard every now and again as each of them tried to assert dominance over the other. It would be hard for Willow — she'd only been living on the boat for a few weeks, and already she was having to give her bedroom up for somebody else. We'd decided that Granny and Mum would share Willow's bedroom, and Willow would sleep with me. Barney would have to make do with the fold down dinette furniture, and Boris would be happy to curl up on a blanket.

Barney pointed into the distance. "Is that a village?" he asked, squinting his eyes against the bright light of the sun.

He was right. It was a village. The riverbanks had been steadily opening up into rolling pastures on one side of the river, as the opposite bank gave way to the foothills of the looming mountains, which had been getting nearer as every minute passed. The slight silver colouration of the rock formations gave us a clue that we were approaching the Silver Mountains which Maeve had told us about.

The small village was comprised of a handful of thatched cottages, some of them with smoke pouring from the chimneys, unchallenged by wind until it reached high into the sky. Children gathered on the sandy beach, shouting greetings and waving at us as we passed.

An elderly man in a fishing coracle paddled out of our path and tipped his hat as he reeled in a trout, which he tossed at his feet to join the others which were soon going to be somebody's dinner.

"I'd have thought it would be a little more magical here," said Barney, as we left the village behind. "Everyone seems to be living normal lives, surely they could magic the fish out of the river if they wanted to?"

"Where would the fun be in that?" said Granny, watching us from the roof of the boat. "These people accept magic as normal, it's more of a novelty to them to do things without magic. That's why hand-made things and food grown from scratch rule the economy. If anybody can conjure up a nice hat, then one that's been handmade is worth a lot more. Possessing a practical skill goes a long way in The Haven. They'll enjoy eating those fish far more than they would if they'd blasted them from the water with a spell."

Barney sipped his wine. "I understand that," he said. "There's something primal about catching your own food. I used to love fishing when I was a child. I kind of miss it."

I smiled. "In the storage compartment on the roof, there's a fishing rod and tackle. It was there when I bought the boat. I've never used it, why don't you try it out?"

Barney's eyes lit up. "I'll catch us some trout!" he said. "We can cook it over a campfire when we moor up for the night!"

He scrambled onto the roof and opened the storage box, the hinges giving a squeaking protest. "I'll use bread as bait," he said, jumping down next to me with the rod and tackle.

As Barney went about assembling the rod, I glanced at the sky. Dusk was falling and the mountains to our left cast a dark shadow over the river. "I'm going to take us ashore when I find a suitable spot," I said. "We're at The Silver Mountains. We'll stay here tonight and if we leave early enough in the morning, we'll be in The City of Shadows by midday."

A LARGE FLAT rock made a perfect natural jetty to moor the boat alongside, and a sandy beach surrounded by ancient trees with an open pasture beyond, made the perfect spot to relax in. The Silver

Mountains rose from the ground about a mile away, and the river gurgled gently as it meandered past. Barney had dug up some worms when it quickly became obvious that the trout in the river weren't big fans of bread, and he'd proudly delivered three fat fish which he'd cleaned and de-scaled ready for cooking.

Mum had been the first to try and light a fire using magic, and then Willow and I had both tried, none of us being able to conjure a single spark from our fingertips.

"Remember what Maeve said," commented Boris, watching us with amusement. "Magic doesn't work in the Silver Mountains. You'll have to do it the old-fashioned way."

With firewood collected and with the use of matches from the boat, we soon had a roaring fire lit, which we sat around watching the fish cook on spits while we drank.

"Would anybody like some elderberry wine?" I offered, as dusk gave way to a starry moonlit sky.

Several bottles of my homemade wine still filled a storage rack aboard the boat, and it seemed that it was only me who truly appreciated its deep natural flavours. The berries had been picked under a full moon, and I was beginning to think that my sense of taste was vastly more advanced than the people's around me.

Boris snorted and looked up, the reflections of the flames dancing in his eyes. "I'll stick with my brandy, thank you, Penelope," he said.

Granny giggled, the brandy she'd been drinking all day cheering her up. "I'm very proud of you, Penelope, you know that, don't you?"

I raised an eyebrow. "I think so."

"You're a trier," she said, "but please don't try your hand at wine making again. That stuff is just filthy."

I ignored everyone's laughter and took a long swallow of wine. It meant more of it for me, and I was sure it was healthier than the array of drinks which everyone else was sipping.

I licked my lips as Barney turned the trout, the skin splitting and browning as the flesh softened. It smelt better than any shop bought fish I'd cooked. Barney glanced behind me at the open grassland at the foot of the mountains. "What are they?" he said, standing up for a better view. "Fireflies? I've never seen a firefly!"

I turned to look. Rising from the grasses and floating from the shadowy silhouettes of trees were dozens of bright lights which dropped, rose and bobbed left and right.

"Do they bite?" said Boris. "They'd better not bite! It's no fun being a goat when there's biting insects around." He looked at Granny. "Did you bring my antihistamine cream, Gladys? I really don't want a repeat of the horsefly incident, and I truly don't relish the thought of you slavering ointment on my… *you know whats* again."

"You should have seen how the bite swelled up," said Granny, smiling at us. "It was like he had three balls, wasn't it, Boris?"

"Thank you, Gladys," said Boris. "You've painted a pretty picture in the minds of my peers."

"You're welcome," said Granny, ignoring Willow's laughter.

"Wait!" said Mum, sitting up straight and staring at the lights which were slowly approaching. "Those aren't fireflies. They're… fairies! I'd heard they lived in The Haven, but I've never seen one before!"

Glee bubbled in my stomach. I'd spent hours as a child searching for fairies at the bottom of Mum's garden. "Fairies! Really?" I said. "Oh, my goddess!"

The lights stopped moving when they were less than ten metres away, and when I squinted I was able to make out the blur of tiny wings through the bright lights. A small female voice called out to us, the vowels in the words rising and falling in pitch like a song. "May we approach?"

Boris leapt to his feet and clamped his rear legs together. "Do you bite?" he asked. "Because if you do, there's a fly swat aboard the boat which Gladys won't be afraid to use!"

A gentle sing-song of murmurs spread between the fairies. "We are not heathens," said the female voice. "We are the fairy clan of the Silver Mountains, and we've been drawn to you by the fragrant perfume you possess."

"That'll be my Chanel number five," said Granny, sniffing her wrist. "I won it in a bingo game on holiday, didn't I, Boris?"

"You pulled the chair from beneath the old man sitting next to you and stole his full house ticket, Gladys," said Boris, "but if we're not splitting hairs, then yes, you won it."

Granny stood up. "You may approach, fairies of the Silver Mountains, and appreciate my perfume further."

More murmuring spread through the swarm of fairies, until two small shapes broke free from the rest of the group and tentatively approached us, heading in my direction. As they neared, their forms became clearer, and I swallowed a delighted giggle when I realised they were just how I'd always imagined fairies to be. One fairy was female, her skin a silvery blue and her tiny dress sparkling with incandescent light, and the other was male, dressed in a silver robe which flowed behind him as he flew. Both wore delicate necklaces of intricate designs, and the female's golden hair was adorned with tiny jewels. Their shimmering light dimmed as they neared me, and their wings buzzed slower as they came to a halt. They stopped inches from my face and studied me, their smiles wide and their small eyes kind. The female bowed in the air. "I am Breena, queen of the Silver Mountain fairies, and this is my king, Trevor."

"Trevor?" said Boris. "Is that even a fairy name? That's the name of a pub landlord, or a used car salesman."

The king span in the air and pointed at Boris. "Your livestock insults me," he said. "Silence the beast. Or he'll be on my spit before this night is over."

"How dare you!" said Granny. "You jumped up little flying bastard! Boris isn't livestock, he's a wonderful and kind spirit."

Breena put a small hand on Trevor. "Don't start arguments, Trevor, or you'll be sleeping on the chaise lounge tonight. Apologise to these people and their goat right away!"

Trevor blushed a pinky red. "I'm sorry," he said, lowering his voice. He cast a glance at the fairies who still hovered a short distance away. "I have to look the part in front of my clan," he nervously explained. "I was showing off. Please accept my humblest apologies."

"Accepted," said Boris.

"Y'all are forgiven," said Granny, slipping into

the American slang she had a habit of using when she was drunk.

Breena raised her voice and addressed the other fairies. "Leave us, clan. We are safe among these kind people and their spirited goat. Go about your night, and know we are safe."

"You'll bring some back for us, won't you?" came a male voice, which was surprisingly deep for such a small life form. "It was me that smelt it in the first place. I should get a share!"

"We'll see!" said Breena. "Now go, and be on the lookout for the horsemen of the deep. They may travel tonight."

The remainder of the clan did as their queen asked and their lights dimmed as they flew into the distance.

"Urm," said Barney, staring at the two fairies with childlike wonder in his eyes. "The horsemen of the what now?"

"Horsemen of the deep," said Trevor, his eyes on my glass. "Dear lady," he said, bringing his eyes to mine. "Would it be rude of me to ask that my queen and I may sample some of the fragrant perfume you possess?"

"Urm," repeated Barney. "Horsemen of the deep? They sound…scary?"

"The worse," said Breena. She dropped from the sky and landed on my knee, standing next to my wine glass. "May I taste some?" she said. "It smells divine."

"It's alcoholic you understand?" I said. "It's a drug."

"Horsemen?" said Barney.

Breena looked up at Barney. "We will speak with you of the horsemen of the deep when our mouths have been wet with the divine liquid captured within this good lady's drinking receptacle."

Trevor dropped from the air and joined his queen on my knee. "I'm gagging for a taste," he said. "It smells so good. May I partake?"

"If fairies can handle alcohol, you're welcome to some," I said.

Trevor laughed. "How else are we supposed to get shit-faced?" he said.

"Language, Trevor!" snapped Breena. "These are refined people. They won't enjoy your foul mouth."

Willow laughed and passed me the lid from a bottle. "Pour some in here for them, Penny," she suggested.

The two fairies fluttered to the floor as I filled the lid and laid it on the sand. Trevor tasted the wine first, dipping his lips to the surface and taking a long swallow. "Delicious," he said. "Who is the winemaker responsible for this drink of the gods?"

Breena took a sip and sighed. "This is fine wine indeed. It was made by the hands of an expert."

"I made it," I said, brimming with pride. "I picked the berries under a full moon!"

Granny snorted, and Barney put an arm around my shoulder.

"I can taste the moonlight," said Trevor, licking his lips. "And a hint of vanilla?"

"Yes!" I said, smiling at Barney. "Can you taste strawberry too? I added a little to sweeten it."

Trevor took another long gulp. "The strawberry makes it what it is, young lady. You possess a remarkable skill."

"Good grief," said Mum. "The wine tastes vile. What's wrong with you, fairies?"

Trevor and Breena ignored her and continued to sip the wine, making appreciative sounds and smiling up at me.

"The fish is done," said Granny. "Who's hungry?"

As Granny passed plates of fish around, including a small portion for Breena and Trevor to share, an echoing horn blew in the distance, startling the two fairies and making the hairs on the back of my neck rise.

"The horsemen of the deep!" shouted Trevor, a tremor in his voice. "Tonight, they hunt!"

CHAPTER FIVE

"We must leave," said Breena, taking a last sip of wine. "Would you be so kind as to send us on our travels with a little of your fine wine? The rest of the clan would truly appreciate it." She flew to an unopened bottle of wine which lay in the sand, and landed on the cork. "This bottle would do nicely. It would last us for days."

"I'm not sure you could carry it," I said. "It's very heavy."

"We are imbued with a strength far greater than our stature would suggest," said Breena. "Transporting this bottle will be an easy feat for us."

"Then you're welcome to it," I said, happy that at last I'd found wine connoisseurs equal to my own high calibre.

The horn sounded again, echoing over the grassland and reverberating in my ears.

Trevor's face whitened. "Hurry," he said, fluttering to the bottle to join his queen. "The horsemen approach! We must take our prize and leave."

Breena withdrew a length of silver strand from a pocket hidden deep in her dress, and proceeded to wrap it around the neck of the bottle while Trevor scanned the dark distance for danger. When the twine was firmly in place, the fairies each held an end, and with no visible exertion, lifted the bottle into the air.

"Wait a cotton-picking minute!" said Granny, leaping to her feet and grabbing the wine bottle, stopping the fairies in mid-flight. "You two aren't going anywhere until you tell us who the horsemen of the deep are! Who do you think you are? Fluttering over here like Mr and Mrs fancy pants, manipulating my granddaughter into handing over her wine, and then leaving when the going gets tough! Not on my nelly! You tell us if we're in danger from these horsemen, or I'll put you both *in* that wine bottle and keep you as pets!"

"You don't want to be her pet," said Boris.

Breena and Trevor tugged on the twine, their wings buzzing so quickly they were barely discernible. "At first, we thought you had come to trade with the horsemen," said Breena, giving the rope another tug. "This is where the horsemen meet the other boat to sell their goods. We assumed you were traders until you lit a fire. The horsemen deal in secrecy, and wouldn't allow a fiery beacon to draw attention to their dealings."

"They are a fearsome people indeed," said Trevor. "They wear clothes of metal and ride great steeds. They hunt us fairies, but have yet to capture one of our type. I would not like tonight to be any different. Give us our wine, and allow us to flee, for I hear the hooves of their stallions in the dry grass. They approach at speed!"

Barney took a step towards the grassland and cupped a hand to his ear. "I hear something," he said. "Like metal clanking."

"Their clothes of protection!" said Trevor, with panic in his voice. "Release the wine, old lady, and let us leave!"

"Let them go, Mother," said Mum. "They're terrified! Poor little things."

Granny reluctantly released the bottle, and the fairies flew away, dragging the wine between them. "Good luck, travellers!" shouted Trevor, as the two lights flitted between trees and were swallowed by the darkness as cloud cover hid the moon. "You will need it!"

Barney grabbed my wrist, pulling me to my feet and dragging me towards the boat. "Come on!" he said, "I'll start the engine. Let's get out of here. I didn't sign up for this mission to end up being murdered by horsemen!"

"Too late," said Boris, staring into the gloom. "They're here. I can smell them."

A loud snort from an animal shrouded in darkness confirmed the horsemen's presence, and the scraping sound of a sword been drawn from a scabbard made my blood run cold. "What do we do?" I said. "Magic won't work here! We're unprotected!"

"Everybody calm down," said Granny. "I'll deal with this." She took a few steps along the beach and spoke into the darkness. "Make yourselves known, vile horsemen!"

A low voice answered, the words muffled and echoing as if spoken from within a helmet. "I wouldn't say we're vile. Some of us may be a little uncouth, but vile is a very harsh word. Take it back at once!"

"Make yourselves shown!" said Granny, "and I'll reconsider my choice of word. Until I see you, I consider you vile."

"Don't antagonise them, Granny," said Willow. "They'll kill us!"

"We'll do no such thing!" said a high-pitched voice.

"Quiet, Bertram!" said the voice in the helmet. "Let me do the talking."

"Sorry," said Bertram, the sincerity evident in his tone.

Barney stepped next to Granny. "We heard a sword being drawn. If you mean us no harm, why are you armed?"

"That was me," said a third voice. "It wasn't a sword being drawn, it was the pipe of peace. It's very long so I store it in a sword scabbard. Sorry for the misunderstanding. It's not the first time its happened."

"Who are you people?" said Granny. "Who are you, horsemen of the deep? Show yourselves!"

"You've been speaking to the fairies, haven't you?" said Bertram. "Only the fairies call us the horsemen of the deep. We live beneath the mountains, yes, but deep? Not really. We live in caves, I'd say we live just below ground level if I'm being totally transparent. Gossiping fairies — they really are a pain."

"Why do you hunt the fairies?" said Granny. "If you are a peaceful people, why would you pursue such small folk?"

"Were the fairies drunk?" said the helmeted person.

"They were on their way to being drunk," said Willow.

"The fairies of the Silver Mountains have a complicated relationship with alcohol," came a voice from the dark. "They like it a little too much, and the only time we chase them is when they steal our mead.

It takes us months to make, and they'd clear us out in a night if we didn't see them off. Those fairies are their own worst enemies, and they leave a terrible mess after a night on the sauce. We once found King Trevor's underwear floating in a vat of our mead. We had to pour the whole batch away."

The clouds finished their journey across the moon, and Granny laughed as the area was bathed in a silver glow. "Stand down, everybody. I think we're safe."

Boris snorted. "Horsemen of the deep, my hairy backside!"

I stifled my own laughter. I was politer than Granny and Boris, but it *was* an amusing sight. Standing in a small semi-circle were three bedraggled donkeys, each carrying a dwarf on its back. Each dwarf wore a mismatched ensemble of dull silver armour, which clanked as they shifted nervously in their saddles. The dwarf in the centre wore a helmet with a small slit to see out of, and the other two wore leather hats, buckled beneath their chins.

"You're dwarfs!" said Granny. "On donkeys! How wonderful!"

"And you're strangers on our land," said the helmeted dwarf, climbing from the saddle and jumping to the ground with a clang of metal. "Please, tell us who you are and what you desire. Are you here to buy our wares?"

Granny smiled. "I am Gladys Weaver, and these people are my family. I apologise for trespassing, sir, we needed somewhere to moor our boat for the night, and this was the perfect spot. We have no wish to buy your wares."

"Sir? I am no sir!" said the dwarf, removing the helmet and bowing. "I am Gretchen the bold of the Silver Mountains."

"You don't look bald," said Boris. "You've got a fine head of hair going on there, madam dwarf."

"Bold!" said Gretchen. "Not bald!"

"My apologies, your boldness," said Boris.

Granny wrung her hands and frowned. "I'm so sorry," she said. "How dare I assume your gender! You *must* believe that this isn't something I do regularly!"

"Be at peace, Gladys Weaver," said Gretchen. "You are forgiven." She addressed the other donkey riders. "Dismount, companions."

The other two dwarfs hopped from their donkeys and stepped into the golden ring of light cast by the fire. "Allow me to introduce Bertram and Ulric," said Gretchen. "My most trusted companions."

Bertram held up a long silver pipe. "It is our custom to welcome strangers with the pipe of peace. Would you do us the honour of joining us for a smoke of some happy herb?"

Granny rubbed her hands together. "I'm in," she

said. "I haven't had a good toke since January the first, nineteen-eighty-four."

"What?" said Mum. "You used to smoke cannabis?"

"It was a one off," said Granny. "Norman and I were celebrating the year we thought George Orwell's book would come true. It never did of course, unfortunately, but the ganja was good, and the living was easy."

"I'd like some too," said Boris. "Beats a cigar."

"Light the pipe of peace, Bertram!" said Gretchen, placing her helmet on the sand near the fire and sitting next to it. "We have new friends to make."

"HAVE THEY HAD TOO MUCH?" said Bertram, throwing the skeleton of the trout he'd eaten into the fire. "They *look* like they've had too much."

"I'd say it looked that way," said Mum, shaking her head.

Gretchen took a long puff on the pipe and blew a perfect circle of smoke, scattering the mosquitoes which had gathered above her head. "We brought the strong stuff," she said. "It's not meant to be taken in such large quantities."

Boris and Granny had both taken drag after long drag on the pipe, while the rest of us had politely refused — with Barney needing to be reminded that he couldn't confiscate the drugs, or press charges against dwarfs of the Silver Mountains. He'd finally relented and sat back to watch Granny and Boris get high. It had been quite the show, and it seemed that they hadn't yet reached the crescendo. They lay in the sand, side by side, a few feet from the fire, Boris's hooves pointing heavenward, and Granny marvelling at the size of the moon. "I feel like I can touch it, Boris," she murmured. "I feel like I can touch the moon."

"You can do anything you put your mind to, Gladys," said Boris, waving a hoof left and right. "You're a special woman."

"Special, my foot," said Mum. "Irresponsible more like."

"Leave them to it," said Willow. "They'll frazzle out and fall asleep soon enough." She looked at Gretchen. "You mentioned selling wares. Are you dealers in the happy herb?"

Barney made a strangled sound in his throat, but managed to compose himself.

"No," said Gretchen. "We don't sell our happy herb. We give that away to anybody who requires it — happiness should be free for all. We sell the metals we mine from the mountains. The metals which give our home its name — the Silver Mountains."

"You sell silver?" said Mum. "You must be rich!"

"No, not silver," said Bertram. "We have no name for the metal we sell." He rapped his knuckles on his armoured chest plate. "This is made from the metal we mine."

"And that's only a recent development," said Ulric, the plait in his long beard swinging dangerously close to the fire as he tossed another log into the flames. "Nobody wanted our metal until a few months ago."

Barney leaned across me. "May I?" he said, forming a fist over Ulric's armour.

Ulric nodded. "Be my guest."

Barney tapped the metal and dragged his fingernail across it. Satisfied, he sat back. "I bet it's heavy to wear, isn't it?" he asked.

"Very heavy," said Gretchen. "But we're strong enough to shoulder the burden."

"It's lead," said Barney. "You really shouldn't be wearing it. It's poisonous if ingested."

"Those rules don't apply here, Barney," I reminded him. "Nobody gets ill in The Haven."

"Well, lead is not very protective either," said Barney, undeterred. "It's too soft to stop a sword. It doesn't make very good armour."

"We do not wear it to deflect the blade of a weapon," said Gretchen. "We wear it to look good."

"It works," said Willow. "You look lovely."

Gretchen couldn't hide the smile that crept over

her face. "How very kind of you to say," she said. "You're certainly people of high standing and fine manners." She passed the pipe of peace to Bertram, and looked at Mum. "Pray tell, what brings such well-mannered folk to our lands?"

"We're investigating a mystery," said Mum. "On behalf of Maeve. We're searching for six witches who have gone missing. They were last seen in the City of Shadows. We plan to arrive there tomorrow and begin our search."

Barney took the opportunity to exercise his policing muscles. "Have you heard or seen anything? Anything suspicious that might help us?"

Gretchen shook her head. "I'm sorry," she said. "Our lands are quiet, we are a simple folk who rarely see strangers, and we stay out of the business of the rest of The Haven. I'm afraid your questions are wasted on us."

"I understand," said Barney. "I'm sure we'll have more luck in the City of Shadows."

Ulric frowned. "Gretchen," he said. "What about those three lady witches who were bound and gagged in the boat of the man who buys our metal?"

Gretchen sighed and rolled her eyes. "I'm sorry," she said to Barney. "Forgive his stupidity." She knocked on Ulric's leather hat with her knuckles. "Hello? Anybody home? He asked if we'd seen anything suspicious, you silly dwarf."

"That is quite suspicious," said Barney, sitting up straight.

"Really?" said Gretchen.

Barney frowned. "You don't think that seeing three women tied up and gagged is suspicious?"

Gretchen's eyes clouded with confusion. "Why would it be? We assumed he was having trouble with his wenches. When our wenches misbehave, we tie them up and gag them until they *can* behave. Doesn't everybody?"

"Aren't you a wench, Gretchen?" said Willow. "What if you misbehaved? Would you be tied up too?"

Ulric and Bertram gasped in unison. "Gretchen is not a wench!" said Bertram, spittle flying from his mouth. "She is a lady! From a high family! How dare you!"

Barney held up a hand. "Stop, please. She didn't mean to be rude. We come from different cultures. In our culture, we don't tie women up, but that's not the point. What you've told us is *very* suspicious... please tell us more. Who is the man on the boat?"

"Don't tie naughty wenches up?" muttered Bertram. "Heathens."

"It was almost half a year ago when he first arrived," said Gretchen. "In a boat, as red as the morning sun. We were happy to sell him our metal — nobody had ever asked us for our metal before."

"Were the captive witches in his boat the first time he visited you?" asked Barney.

"Oh no," said Bertram. "He came a few more times before that night."

"What does he want your lead for?" asked Barney, his notebook and pencil in hand.

"He does not tell us," said Gretchen. "He buys a tonne in weight each time he visits."

"How does he pay for your metal?" said Willow. "With gold?"

"We don't swap metal for metal. We have no use for gold," said Ulric. "We are paid in condiments that are hard to come by in The Haven. Spices, pepper, mustard... all the things that finish a nice meal off. The mustard is particularly good — especially on a salt baked trout. His payments have certainly changed our diets."

"They *certainly* have," said Bertram, rubbing a hand over his armour protected belly. "I've put pounds on since I discovered spicy food, and doesn't my donkey know it."

"He pays for the metal you've risked life and limb to mine from the mountains, with spices?" said Mum. "That hardly seems a fair swap."

"Not just condiments," said Gretchen. "He pays us with his promise too. The promise that when he acquires the one true power, he will bestow upon us such glory that the name of the dwarfs of the Silver

Mountains will be forever enshrined in the folklore of The Haven. We will be a people to be reckoned with — his words, not mine, although I do like the way they roll off the tongue."

"Power?" said Barney. "What power?"

Gretchen shrugged. "We only know what he tells us."

"One true power!" said Mum. "Hilda warned us of a power! Her vision was correct!"

"Does the man have hair as black as coal?" said Barney, recalling Hilda's prophecy.

"I do not know. He shrouds himself in a hooded cloak as black as the depths of the night sky," said Gretchen. "But if he matches his clothes with his hair, there's a good chance his hair *is* black."

"And the witches in the boat?" said Willow. "Can you tell us anything about them?"

"It was a few weeks ago, and it was a very dark night," said Bertram. "They were chained up in a corner of the boat's hold. We didn't really pay them much attention. We assumed they'd been *very* mischievous. We helped the man load his metal and went on our way."

"How is it possible to imprison a witch?" said Barney. "Surely they could use magic to escape?"

"Not if the man had more powerful magic than the witches," said Mum. "It would be easy. He wouldn't need chains; a simple spell would capture them. The chains were to stop them escaping when he brought them here, where no magic can be used."

"Do you know where he takes his metal?" said Willow. "Do you know where he took the witches?"

"He speaks of a ten-hour journey, and he comes from, and returns west along the river," said Gretchen. "I would guess that he travels to the City of Shadows."

"We should leave now," said Barney. "Hearing of witches chained up in a boat has made this whole thing seem far more urgent!"

"The lamp on my boat isn't bright enough for night travel," I said, "and we can't use a magical light until we're clear of these mountains. It would be far too dangerous. Besides, I don't think we'd have much luck getting Boris and Granny aboard."

"What on earth are they doing?" said Mum.

At the rim of the circle of light cast by the fire, Granny stood on tiptoes, her fingertips grasping at the air above her head. "I can't reach it, Boris," she wailed. "I can't touch the moon!"

Boris reared up on his hind legs, his front hooves waving. "Me neither, Gladys. I can't touch it either. There's only one thing for it. You must ride me to the moon!"

"You're a genius, Boris, a genius," murmured Granny.

"Thank me when our feet touch cheese, Gladys,"

said the goat. "Climb aboard, dear lady, and ride me hard and fast. Ride me like there's no tomorrow!" He dug all four hooves firmly into the sand and tilted his head rearward. "Use my horns to steer, and trust in my abilities, Gladys, for I am your steed tonight. I will fly you to the moon."

"Oh, Boris," said Granny, swinging a leg over the goats back and taking a curled horn in each hand. "I'm to be the first astronaut in my family, and it's all thanks to you. I'll never forget this night."

Boris looked skyward. "Settle in, Gladys, for the flight will be long and arduous."

Granny leaned forward and lifted her knees, allowing Boris to take her full weight. The goat shuddered for a moment, before emitting a wailing gasp of pain and collapsing into the sand, his legs akimbo and his head at an odd angle.

"Fly, beautiful Boris, fly!" shouted Granny, slamming her heels into Boris's quivering hind-quarters. "Make haste!"

Boris took a rattling breath. "Are we there yet, Gladys?"

"Almost, Boris, almost. Fly faster!"

"It's hard to breathe," gasped Boris, his snout slipping below the sand.

"It's the altitude," said Granny. "You'll soon get used to it."

Barney leapt to his feet and crossed the sand in

three long strides. He lifted Granny from the back of the goat, ignoring her protests and dodging her flailing fists. She fell to the sand and stared into the night sky. "So close," she murmured. "Yet so far."

Boris took a deep breath as Barney rubbed his flanks. He blew chunks of sand from his nostrils and sighed. "We'll try again tomorrow, Gladys," he said.

"Tomorrow," repeated Granny. "Sleep à la carte with me tonight, Boris, we'll dream of flying to the moon."

Boris giggled. "You mean al fresco, dear Gladys, and I'd be happy to share the blanket of stars with you."

Gretchen stood up. "Bertram, put that pipe of peace away," she said. "It's done enough damage for one night." She smiled at me. "We shall leave you now. Good luck with your quest." She glanced at Boris and Granny before sliding her helmet over her head. "I fear you'll need all the luck of the Silver Mountains."

The dwarfs mounted their donkeys, and will a final farewell, rode into the night, their laughter echoing across the plains.

"Help me get Granny aboard, Barney," I said. "I'm not leaving her in the sand."

Mum and Willow helped Boris stumble to the boat as Barney and I each slid a hand beneath

Granny's armpits and helped her to her feet. "Come on," I said. "It's time for bed."

"I've got a secret," mumbled Granny.

"Come on, Gladys," urged Barney. "It's getting cold and the fire will go out soon. I've never seen anyone get so stoned before."

"Do you want to know why I won't take my dementia cure?" slurred Granny.

"Why?" I said, supporting her as she tripped over a log.

"I love him," she said. "I love Boris. Not the goat you must understand — I'm a progressive, but even I draw the line somewhere. I love the man within him — Charleston Huang, and when I take my cure and he leaves the body of the goat, he'll leave me for ever. He's in his sixties, and I'm at least… ten years older. He won't want to be with me. I'll lose my soul mate." Her eyes slid closed and her breathing became laboured.

"Wake up, Granny!" I said. "What do you mean you love him?"

"Watcha mean?" she mumbled. "Watcha talking about? Are there munchies on the boat? I'm hungry."

CHAPTER SIX

*W*e'd been traveling for almost four hours when Granny finally woke up, the remains of the three chocolate muffins she'd eaten the night before lining her lips, and her eyes bloodshot. "My head hurts," she said, emerging from Willow's bedroom and approaching the narrow galley kitchen where I was preparing hot drinks. "Why is it you only become ill from over indulgence in The Haven? It doesn't seem fair."

"Probably so people think twice before doing it again," I said. "Sit down, I'll make you a coffee."

"Where's everyone else?" she said.

"Willow's driving the boat and the others are on the roof, sunbathing. We're half way to the city of Shadows, they wanted to relax a little before we arrive," I said, handing Granny a mug.

Granny sipped the coffee and smiled. "That stuff the dwarfs gave us was far stronger than the weed me and Norman smoked back in eighty-four, all we did back then was dance to Norman's favourite song — Pass the Dutchie — and eat too much cheese. I can't remember *what* I did last night!"

"I can help you out with that," I said, "you told me and Barney that —"

Granny out a finger to her lips. "And I don't want to know, thank you, sweetheart."

"But —"

"No buts, Penelope," snapped Granny. "I *don't* want to know."

The thud of a skull on a low door frame, followed by a swear word that made Granny wince, marked Barney's arrival into the belly of the boat. He rubbed his head as he smiled at Granny. "Morning, Gladys," he said. "Did you have a good time last night?"

"I'm sure I did," said Granny, "but as I've being telling Penny — I don't want to know what happened last night."

"Fair enough," said Barney, giving me a knowing glance. "Anyway, I've had an idea. We need to summon Maeve. She should know about what the dwarfs told us. She's almost like my police superior if you think about it, and superiors should always be informed of a breakthrough in a case."

"Breakthrough?" said Granny with a raised

eyebrow. "What breakthrough? Why don't I know anything about this development?"

"You were otherwise occupied when the dwarfs gave us some information," I said with a smile.

Granny put her mug down. "Well fill me in then."

Without speaking over one another, Barney and I repeated the story the dwarfs had told us. When we'd finished, Granny nodded at Barney. "I agree, Barney," she said. "Maeve must be told. Knowing that three witches were being held captive in a boat changes everything. I must admit that I thought the six witches had simply decided to become outsiders — there are communities of people throughout The Haven who live in places similar to The Silver mountains, where magic doesn't work. They shun society and they shun magic, but I'm now led to believe the witches are being held against their will... or worse. Summon her, Barney, and we can only hope that Derek doesn't come along for the ride. Ghastly man that he is."

WILLOW STAYED ABOVE DECK, driving the boat, as the rest of us gathered in the living area. Barney remained standing, with the stone Maeve had given him in his hand, and the rest of us sat on the dinette furniture, with Boris at Granny's feet.

"What do I do?" said Barney, inspecting the small black stone.

"Just think of her," said Mum, "and she'll appear."

Barney closed his eyes and wrinkled his nose. He muttered Maeve's name under his breath, and cautiously opened his eyes. "Is she here yet?"

His answer came in the form of a swirl of smoke which materialised before him. Mum leapt up and turned on the extraction fan above the small gas cooker as Maeve took on her solid form and smiled. "You require my presence?" she said.

"Is Derek not with you today?" said Granny. "You two seem to have been joined at the hip recently."

"Derek is otherwise occupied, Gladys," said Maeve. She lowered herself gracefully into the comfy wicker chair opposite us, threading a hand through her golden hair. "With your sister."

"What's Eva doing with that hideous man?" snapped Granny. "The silly woman! She should know better."

"You don't give Derek *or* your sister enough credit, Gladys," said Maeve. "Eva is wise, and Derek isn't as bad as you like to assume he is." She looked at Barney. "Why did you summon me, lawman? Surely not so that Gladys can question me about Derek's whereabouts?"

"No, of course not," said Barney, retrieving his

notebook from his pocket. "We have information about three of the missing witches."

Maeve's playful expression moulded into concern. "Speak," she said abruptly.

For the second time that day, Barney retold the story. When he'd finished speaking, Maeve leaned back in her seat with her eyes closed and let out a long breath.

"Well?" said Granny. "What should we do?"

"We should hurry to the City of Shadows," said Maeve. "I have great concern for the missing witches. I have a home in the city, we'll gather there and formulate a plan."

***

THE STRETCH of river which led into the city was busier than any I'd seen in the mortal world. It seemed that not all of The Haven was a vision of calm tranquillity after all. Boats vied for mooring spots along the quays and wharfs which made up the port area of the city, and traders transported wares from their boats onto the dockside where horses and carts waited to take them away. We could have been in London during the eighteen-hundreds, and the sight of a young boy running alongside the river pushing a hoop in front of him with a stick, solidified that vision. The abundance and array of different colours and types of boats immediately shot down any plans I'd formulated of simply looking for a red boat and finding the person responsible for taking the missing witches.

Mouth-watering cooking aromas filled the air, and a large market area was loud with the sound of traders shouting over each other as they each attempted to attract customers with their bargains. It was a completely different haven than the one I'd witnessed so far, and I looked forward to exploring the city.

Maeve guided me past the busy port area, pointing to a channel of water which took us to a secluded harbour. I maneuvered *The Water Witch* into the mooring which Maeve indicated, and cut the engine as a man on the wharf side caught the ropes which Barney tossed ashore, and tied us off.

"This is a rarely used harbour," said Maeve. "Traders don't use it. Your boat will be safe here, and more to the point, so will you."

"Secure from what?" said Willow. "I've always thought The Haven was a safe place."

"It used to be," said Maeve. "And the countryside still is, but in recent decades some people have tired of the old magical ways. They miss the world left behind when they came to live in The Haven, and have sought to recreate it here. A little too well for my liking. Even I have no control over some cities and towns."

"Why don't you take back control?" said Boris, navigating the narrow gangplank which a dock worker had laid between the boat's hull and the low stone quay. "It's your haven."

"I'm not a dictator," said Maeve. "And I have no wish to be. I believe in allowing people to achieve their own destiny, even if I don't always agree with that destiny. If I was to rule The Haven with an iron fist, I'd be no better than the people who tried to burn me alive at the stake." She followed Boris along the plank and drew her hood over her head as she stepped onto the quay. "I will hide my identity. Many people in the city reject authority, and if you're seen with me they may not trust you when you begin searching for our lost witches. Your questions will remain unanswered."

"Aren't you going to help us search for the witches?" said Granny, slapping a man's hand away as he attempted to help her off the plank. The elderly man took a startled step backwards and narrowly saved himself from slipping into the gap between boat and land.

"I'll be more of a hindrance than a help," said Maeve. "People are wary of me, and will not seek to aid me. Come to my home, and I'll tell you more about the city and suggest some folk you may want to speak with. Some people in the city have their ears closer to the ground than others."

"Like the dwarfs!" said Granny, lifting a hand for a high five, which everybody ignored.

A drably coloured carriage, drawn by four black horses, drew to a halt above us at the top of the narrow set of slippery stone steps which led from the mooring to the main quayside.

"Our transport awaits," said Maeve.

"It's not very grand, is it?" said Granny, with an upturned nose.

"I don't want to draw attention to us, Gladys Weaver," said Maeve. "Come, climb aboard, everybody. My home is a short drive away."

The carriage was cramped, but everybody managed to find a seat. Barney's thigh pressed against mine and Granny put a hand on Boris's head, lazily twirling her finger through his hair. As the goat gave a contented sigh, Barney nudged me and winked. With a roll of my eyes, I looked away from Boris and Granny and instead concentrated on the streets of The City of Shadows which moved past the window next to me like a strange period drama on the TV screen. The period drama I was watching outside was a mismatch of historical eras, with some people dressed in clothes which I guessed had been practical in the medieval period, and others dressed in clothes which were of the same style as the ones I wore. Men in world-war two soldier's uniforms sat outside a tavern drinking beer and three women in dresses straight out of the nineteen-sixties chatted to them, batting their eyelids and sipping cocktails. I reminded myself that people in the magical dimension had been arriving for centuries, and modern witches from the mortal world visited regularly, bringing their own styles with them. I gave a low giggle as I compared the view outside the carriage to the fancy dress party Willow and I had attended the summer before. Willow had dressed as a sexy pirate, and I'd hidden my figure with a Pikachu outfit. The unflattering costume had not only ruined any chance I'd had of attracting any male attention, but had also been responsible for three embarrassing falls on the dance floor, and at least four pounds of weight loss due to excessive perspiration and a small mouth hole through which I could only squeeze the tiniest of finger foods.

Street vendors cooking all manner of food lined the dusty pavements, and I licked my lips as the sweet aroma of barbecued meat filled the small carriage. A small tree filled park bustled with people, and children laughed as they watched a man on stilts juggling five balls, his vintage clown costume a throwback to a time long ago. The City of Shadows was not named for the dark underbelly which it undoubtedly possessed, but took its name from the shadows which were always cast due to the year-round sun, and true to its name, the city was awash with sunlight which lifted my spirits.

"It's a beautiful city," I said, to no one in particular.

"It has its beauty and it has its ugly side," said Maeve, "but I think you'll enjoy your time here."

The sprightly clip-clop of the horse's hooves slowed in tempo as the driver took a turn, causing us all to lurch to the left. "We're here," said Maeve, as the carriage passed through a set of tall wrought iron gates. "Welcome to my home in the city."

CHAPTER SEVEN

aeve's home was impressive. It wasn't the castle on the hill which I'd been expecting a witch who was powerful enough to conjure up a magical dimension to live in, but it was most certainly worthy of a person of great importance.

The driveway snaked through perfect lawns and tall trees, and the large house, built in the style of an Edwardian manor, was guarded by stone lions and dragons. Two flights of steps led to the marble pillared entrance, and a short portly woman dressed in a flowing black dress stood at the top to greet us. "Miss Maeve!" she said. "It's a pleasure to have you home. When I knew you were arriving with guests, I ordered the cooks to roast a whole pig. I trust you're all hungry?"

Maeve handed the carriage driver a silver coin, and waved at the red-faced woman. "Hello, Mildred," she said, leading us up the steps. "I'm sure we could all do with a bite to eat, thank you."

The large woman hurried into the house, clapping her hands and barking orders. "Prepare the dining room," she shouted. "Miss Maeve is home! Chop, chop!"

"I wish they wouldn't treat me this way," said Maeve. "The staff were all servants in the mortal world, and they seem to enjoy continuing to perform their jobs in this world. I don't enjoy the fuss, but they insist on it."

"They know their place," said Granny, handing a butler her cardigan and patting him on the head as he bowed. "Keep them on their toes, Maeve. If they sense any weakness from you, they'll be rifling through your family silver before you can say, *shine my Sunday shoes, you common piece of shi* —"

"Mother!" snapped Mum. "Have some respect!"

"They don't want respect," said Granny. "It would only confuse them. They're simple folk with no self-esteem."

"This way, please," said Maeve, frowning at Granny and leading us across the large entrance hall, her heels clicking on the granite floor. "Let's eat, and discuss our missing witches."

AFTER FRESHENING up in one of the many bathrooms, I joined the others in the large dining room. A long mahogany table took centre stage, and the tall walls were decorated with large paintings and intricate embroideries, some of them over six-feet in length. A crystal chandelier hung from the ceiling, the candles which gave off the light burning brightly, and a tall unlit fireplace took up most of the space in the wall opposite the doorway.

I took my seat between Barney and Willow as Matilda wheeled in a long wooden stand on which lay a whole pig, its skin a crispy gold and its body surrounded by cooked vegetables and a large pot of what smelt like the finest gravy I'd ever shared a room with. Matilda began slicing the pork, and Boris closed his eyes, making a sobbing sound. "It seems so cruel now I'm in the body of an animal," he whimpered. "Poor, poor pig."

Boris sat on a smaller table which had been drawn alongside the main table to perform as a makeshift seat, and Granny pulled it a little nearer to her side. "There, there," she said. "You don't have to eat any, Boris. I'm sure the cooks can make you something else." She raised an enquiring eyebrow in Maeve's direction.

"Of course!" said Maeve. "What would you like, Boris? Salad… grass?"

Boris shook his head. "No. The cooks have gone to so much trouble — it would be rude of me. I'll put my feels aside and eat what's been prepared."

"I wouldn't hear of it," said Maeve. "Nobody should eat out of guilt! I'll get Matilda to bring you in some lovely hay, and maybe a nice rosy red apple."

"Of course, Miss Maeve," beamed Matilda. "It would be my pleasure."

"I want the pork," murmured Boris, a spark of annoyance in his eyes. "Give me some pork."

Granny scowled. "You fickle little attention seeking bast —"

Willow and Mum gasped, and Barney blushed.

"Apple sauce, sir?" said Matilda, her voice loud enough to drown out Granny's profanities.

"That would be divine, lovely Matilda," said Boris. "And maybe a nice bit of crackling? From the belly of the beast?"

"Your wish is my desire, sir," said Matilda, piling Boris's plate high with food.

Boris tucked in, gravy dripping from his beard, as everyone else was served and Matilda left the room, pushing the pig before her. "Ring when you'd like coffee, Miss Maeve," she said as she left the room.

The food was delicious, and nobody spoke for a

few minutes as the clank of silver cutlery on fine china echoed around the room, interspersed by sounds of appreciation and the occasional belch from Granny, who shifted the blame onto Boris with covert sideways jerks of her head. When the plates were empty, and Matilda had wheeled in coffee and the drinks cabinet for Boris, Maeve leaned forward. "If everyone's had their fill of food, allow me to make a suggestion as to how you approach the search for the lost witches."

Barney slid his notebook and pencil from his pocket. "That would be a great help," he said. "It's always a good idea to have local knowledge."

"If it's local knowledge you want, lawman," said Maeve, "then you need look no further than a particularly shady business premises in the city. *The Nest of Vipers* — a tavern, as the name suggests, has a reputation for quenching the thirsts of some of the less desirable characters in the city. You'll find it near the clock tower. Be cautious though, and don't mention my name. You'll get no help if you do. A conversation with some of the tavern's patrons may point you in the right direction"

"Got it," said Barney, writing in his book.

"I must admit to having a great feeling of unease," said Maeve, "and not just for the safety of the lost witches, but for The Haven itself."

"Why?" said Mum.

"The power that the dwarfs told you of, and that

Hilda spoke of," said Maeve, "troubles me immensely." She drained her coffee cup and sat back. "When I created The Haven," she said, "there was nothing here. I had to magic a home to live in, and as time went on and more witches arrived, we began building our homes — we were prouder of homes we'd constructed with our own hands than homes conjured up by magic." She paused for a moment, deep in thought. "And then I found it."

"Found what?" said Boris, pushing an empty saucer towards Granny who topped it up with brandy from the impressive drinks cabinet.

Maeve frowned. "The only building in this land that nobody built or conjured into existence. A castle... hidden in the mountains to the west, overlooking a great lake. It's a beautiful building, and one I tried to enter repeatedly, but alas — I couldn't."

"You can't get into it?" said Willow. "Why?"

"It is protected by a spell," said Maeve. "A spell so powerful, that even I, the creator of The Haven, cannot break."

"If you didn't create the castle or cast the spell... who did?" asked Mum, reaching for a third biscuit from the plate Matilda had supplied with the drinks.

Maeve shook her head. "I do not know, but I found a stone nearby, hidden from view, with an inscription gouged into its surface."

"What was written on the stone?" said Granny.

Maeve sighed. "It says, *the holder of the one true power will come from the east bearing a jewel, and the castle will be claimed. Only the true ruler of this land can break the spell.*"

"You're the true ruler of The Haven, Maeve," said Mum. "You created it. There must be a mistake."

"I thought as much, Maggie," said Maeve, "but things are happening — witches are vanishing and people are speaking of a power that only I should know of — I put my own spell around the castle *and* the existing spell, so nobody else can get near to it — nobody but me knows of that stone or the castle, I'm the only person to have been there, and the only person who knows of its existence." She looked around the table. "Until now, but I know in my soul that I can trust each one of you with this information... even you, Gladys Weaver."

"Your words cut me deep, Maeve," said Granny. "How rude. How very rude, and to think I could have been back in Wickford, showing off in my new Range Rover and tending to my chickens, but yet I chose to come here and help you solve the mystery of the lost witches! I'm offended, Maeve. Off-en-ded."

Electric buzzed in the air around Maeve, and her whole demeanour changed. "As offended as I was when you chopped down the magic rose bush, or fought a guerrilla war against Derek, in the west? The poor man had to move to the east and change his name from The Copper Haired Wizard of The West, because of you, Gladys. You have a colourful history in The Haven, Gladys, and you should be pleased that I ever lifted your banishment and allowed you back in. The fact that I now trust you is a bonus indeed. I even gave you the cure for your dementia, which for a reason known only to you, you still haven't taken."

Granny filled Boris's saucer again, her cheeks showing the gentle blush of embarrassment. "My apologies, Maeve," she said. "I spoke out of turn."

Barney gave me a sideways glance. We both knew why Granny had backed down so quickly, but we'd promised one another we'd keep it a secret between the two of us. If Granny still hadn't taken the cure by the time we got back to Wickford, we would confront her. It wasn't fair on Charleston to be trapped inside the body of a goat because Granny had fallen in love with him, although he looked pretty happy lapping up the brandy which Granny was feeding him. He'd last another few days.

Granny pointed at the wall behind Maeve, completely changing the subject. "Who's that handsome hunk of man?" she said, gazing at a portrait of a young muscular man with thick dark hair. "I wouldn't throw him out of bed for playing the bagpipes."

Mum bristled. She had an irrational dislike of the Scottish, and the image of a man playing their national musical instrument in a bed had obviously hit a nerve.

"Granny!" laughed Willow. "He's far too young for you! I wouldn't mind meeting him, though!"

"He's nothing special," grunted Boris.

Maeve turned to look at the portrait. "You've met him, Willow" she said, turning to face Granny. A smile played on her lips. "That's the man who's currently wooing your sister, Gladys," she said. "That handsome *hunk* of man is Derek."

Granny got to her feet and hurried to the painting. "Derek does not have black hair," she protested, standing below the oil painted portrait and pushing her glasses further up her nose, as if by moving the lenses closer to her eyes she would make sense of what she was seeing. "He has dirty blond hair, which is never styled very well. He's always reminded me of a scruffy scarecrow, and the man in this picture reminds me of a lovely librarian, or a high-class gigolo."

"Those two professions don't even belong in the same sentence," said Boris. "Anyway, he's not that good looking, his nose is too small for his eyes."

Granny looked down at the goat who stood next to her, a little unsteady on his feet after downing nearly half a bottle of brandy. "Jealousy will get you nowhere, Boris," she said. "Anyhow, if the portrait is of Derek, then I feel sick for even suggesting he's good looking. Disgusting man that he is."

Maeve gave a gentle laugh. "I can assure you it's Derek," she said. "He dyes his hair with magic these days, but that's what he looked like when he was first granted his haven entry spell, Gladys, many hundreds of years ago. And that's how he looks right now as he takes your sister to his home in the east. Derek is shy of reverting to his younger age in front of most people, but not when it comes to impressing pretty young ladies like Eva."

"The little harlot!" said Granny. "She knows Derek and I don't get along, and she's chosen to go gallivanting with him! Why she'd want to go to the east with him, I'll never know, only farmers and failures live in the east!"

"Farmers?" said Willow, "why would farmers live in the east?"

"The climate," said Mum, eating the last of the biscuits. "It's wet and humid in the east, but dry and hot in most of the west. It's no good trying to grow crops in the west without magic. The east is where most of the crops are grown. I'm not sure why your grandmother mentioned failures, though."

Granny shrugged. "Farmers — failures, same difference."

"Derek enjoys growing things from seed," said Maeve. "He's a simple man really, who got dragged into the politics of The Haven. I hope he and Eva enjoy themselves, Gladys. I'm sure they both deserve some happiness. Anyway, the east is a nice place to live. I have a home there myself, as does Hilda. She likes the peacefulness of the hills, it helps her to hone her visions."

"Good for Hilda," said Granny, "and Derek and Eva are welcome to each other. They can be farmers together. I always was the classiest sister."

"Class comes in all types," said Maeve, with a wink in my direction. "Would you all like to see more of my paintings? I keep the best ones in the library."

"I'd love to," said Willow.

"I'm quite the art critic," said Boris, with a belch. "I'd like to cast my eye over your pieces, Maeve."

"I'm sure you would," said Granny, running her eyes along Maeve's slim figure.

"Then follow me this way, please," said Maeve, heading for the doorway. "You'll like my library."

CHAPTER EIGHT

*T*he library smelt of leather and old books, which was no surprise, as long rows of old books lined the tall shelves, and leather furniture provided the seating. The huge book shelves filled two of the four walls and four sliding ladders made it easy to pick a book from even the highest shelf. The wall opposite the doorway was reserved for art, and Maeve had made sure to utilise every available piece of space with oil painted portraits, landscapes and stunning waterscapes.

"Impressive," said Boris, wandering across the thick carpet and gazing up at the pieces. "Very impressive."

Willow and I focused on the books, craning our necks to scan the shelves, noticing books we recognised from our world, and books with titles such as *'Portal Travel - A Step Into The Unknown,'* which had obviously been written by an author from The Haven. Maeve stood at my side, smiling as I scanned the thousands of book spines. "I'm happy to see that you two appreciate books," she said. "Books are the sturdy foundation that any advanced civilisation is built upon."

"I love books," said Willow, opening a leather-bound tome on ancient spell-craft and pressing her nose into the yellowed pages. "Mmmm," she murmured, closing the book and sliding it back into place on a shelf. "You can't beat the smell of old paper."

"My word!" shrieked Mum, from the other side of the room. "You have a macabre taste in art, Maeve."

"I think it's wonderful," said Boris, gazing at the wall above him. "It speaks of death and rebirth, and the evil that mankind is capable of. It's a fine work of art indeed."

"It reminds me of where I came from," said Maeve, crossing the room. "Although on some days I'd rather not remember."

Willow and I followed her and stood beneath the painting that had shocked Mum. It wasn't as macabre as Mum's reaction had made me believe, but it wasn't the sort of painting I'd have liked on my wall either. Framed in dark wood and painted with an accomplished hand, the painting filled a huge portion of the wall, with life sized figures filling the canvas. The painting portrayed Maeve as she burned at the stake, and I gave her arm a gentle squeeze as a tear bulged in the corner of her eye. "It hurts every time I look at it," she said, laying a soft hand over mine. "But it serves a purpose. It reminds me of why I don't wish to become a dictator in my own land. Nasty things happen to good people when one person has too much power."

"It's barbaric," said Barney. "Truly barbaric, and to think that this was allowed to happen in the country I enforce the law in, it makes me shudder."

The painting showed Maeve tied to a stake surrounded by a tall pyre of logs. Bright orange flames licked at her legs and her face was contorted in pain as people in the background looked on in horror, with some women covering their children's faces, and men staring at the ground in helpless despair. The second life sized figure in the painting couldn't have been more different than the onlookers in the way he was portrayed as behaving. A tall black hat hid most of his long dark hair, and his face showed a horrific expression of glee, his teeth bared in a savage smile and his eyes wide and excited as he watched a woman burn.

"What an evil man," said Granny.

"The Witch-finder General," said Maeve, her

hand still on mine, her fingers gripping me tight. "He was responsible for searching out and killing many witches, most of them with a trial which was only ever going to end in a verdict of guilt, quickly followed by the punishment of death by drowning or burning."

"Dark times indeed," murmured Boris. "Dark times indeed."

Barney leaned closer to the painting, his height affording him a better view than the rest of us. "There's something about his eyes," he said, "something very evil."

Maeve's fingers closed tighter. "Not only was his cruelty rarer than most people's," she said, "but so were his eyes. Look closely, lawman, beneath his brows, and you'll see his eyes are of different colours. He claimed they were a gift from God which gave him the ability to see witches where nobody else could. Those eyes were the last thing I saw before I closed my own and prepared to die."

"You're right," murmured Barney, moving even nearer to the painting. "One eye is brown and one is green."

"The artist did a good job," said Maeve. "It was painted by a male witch who watched my near demise. He came into The Haven not long after my fortuitous escape from the jaws of fiery death. He told me that the Witch-finder General dug through the ashes of the pyre for one full day and one full night, searching for my ashes and bones, desperate to prove that God had not saved me from death as the other onlookers believed when I vanished in a flash of light."

"But really, you'd been able to cast a spell so powerful that you created this wonderful land," said Boris. "Remarkable."

"And purely fate's doing," said Maeve. "I was prepared to die. Using magic to save myself would have resulted in more witches and innocent people dying when the Witch-finder took his revenge. I did not cast the spell, my magic did that for me."

"How awful," said Maggie. "We witches don't know how good we have it these days."

"I'm glad it is that way," said Maeve, finally releasing my hand and wiping a tear from her cheek. "And I'm happy to be able to offer refuge in this land to anyone who should need it. The Haven has saved many a witch's life in the centuries since it was created."

The heavy door creaked behind us, and Matilda stepped into the room. "Do you require anything else, Miss Maeve? It's getting late and I should be leaving for home."

Maeve's mood lifted. "No, Matilda. I need no more from you. Go now, and thank you for what you did for us today, the pork was heavenly, and your service was divine."

Matilda performed a half bow, and left the room with a smile. "Thank you, Miss Maeve."

Maeve glanced at a window high in the wall. "It is nearly dark, perhaps you should be getting back to your boat. I will be gone by the morning. I have my own investigations to carry out. While you good people search for the missing witches, I will be scouring the land for information on the great power that has been spoken of. Should you discover anything, do not hesitate to summon me again. I will come quickly." She turned her back on the paintings. "I'll summon my carriage."

"I don't know about everyone else," I said, "but I'd like to walk."

Barney agreed. "That's how you get the feel of the pulse of a town — you walk the beat. I'll walk with you, Penny."

"As will I," said Boris.

With all of us in agreement that an evening walk through the city would be pleasant, we said our good-byes to Maeve on the steps outside the house, and promised to keep her updated about any develop-ments in our search for the witches. Maeve had insisted we took the pouch of coins she offered us, explaining that currency would go a lot further than magical ability in a city such as the one we were in.

"Do we know the way?" said Boris, as we reached the end of the driveway and followed the dusty road downhill. "I didn't take much notice on the way here, but to be fair on myself, I couldn't see out of the carriage window."

"I offered you a place on my lap, Boris," said Granny, watching an elderly man light a street-lamp with a spell cast from the tip of a wand. "You chose to sit on the floor at my feet."

"I'm way ahead of you all," said Willow, walking half a pace in front of us. "It's so easy to use magic here. I've cast a spell of direction — and used the boat as a beacon, it will lead me right to it."

"Or we could just head in that direction," said Barney, pointing at the twinkling lights of the docks below us. "Basic cub scout skills — walk downhill until you find water."

Willow gave Barney a playful slap on his arm. "Spoilsport," she said. "I don't get to use magic much in the mortal world. Let me have my fun!"

"Lead the way," said Barney. "I'm sure your way will take us via a quicker route than I would have."

After a few minutes of walking the quiet streets soon gave way to the bustle of city life at night. Smells of food and the upbeat sounds of live music excited my senses, and I leaned into Barney as he slipped his arm through mine. "I love it here," he said, watching a man playing an accordion outside a small tavern. "Everything is so... simple."

Fireworks exploded in the sky above the city and Granny clapped her hands as the explosions morphed into the glowing shapes of a huge dragon and a phoenix, which flew into the night together, heading for the distant snow-capped mountains which glowed silver beneath the moon. "Magical pyrotechnics!" she said, laughing. "You don't get those in Wickford!"

"And a good job too," said Mum, ever the realist. "I've heard stories about those firework creatures causing untold damage. They don't just fizzle out like a catherine wheel, you know! They fly around for weeks, setting fire to hay-barns and scaring animals."

"Lighten up, you miserable lump of lard," said Granny. "Breathe the air, and feel the magic running through you. If I didn't have dementia I'd launch a few of my own fireworks. My griffin would put that phoenix to shame, *and* give the dragon a run for its money too."

The crowds of people jostling for space became louder as we reached the centre of the city, and the malty aroma of real ales pouring from the open doors of numerous taverns caused Boris's nose to twitch. "Anyone for a taste of the local brew?" he suggested. "Gladys... I'm sure you'd like a snifter or two?"

"You don't need to ask me twice," said Granny.

"I'm in," said Barney. "Why not?" He pointed

across the wide street. "We'll go in there for a drink," he said, "we may as well mix business with pleasure."

"The Nest of Vipers," said Boris. "Maeve warned us it was frequented by ruffians; do we really want to go in there tonight?"

Granny rubbed her hands together and scurried towards the open door. "Just you try and stop me, Boris," she said. "I'm yet to meet a ruffian who could scare Gladys Weaver!"

Boris trotted after her, narrowly avoiding being run over by a man on horseback who veered right at the last moment. "Keep your goat out of the road!" the rider shouted, as Barney and I walked hand in hand after Boris, with Mum and Willow behind us.

The Nest of Vipers looked a friendly enough place from the outside. Even the snakes which formed the letters on the hanging name sign were smiling as their tongues searched the air, and warm light spilled from the two large windows. The hum of conversation and music grew louder as we approached the open door, and a man sitting on a bench outside tipped his hat in our direction.

Inside the tavern, a roaring fire burned in the large hearth at the far end of the room, and the long tables were occupied by a diverse crowd of people, some of who looked up as we made our way towards the bar. A small raised stage in a corner took the place of the customary juke-box I was used to seeing in the pubs at home, and the three-man band who sat on it played folk music on guitars and an accordion, accompanying a beautiful woman who sang in a buttery voice which sent shivers along my spine.

A large man laughed as Boris passed the table he sat at with a dwarf and three women, all of them drinking foaming beers from earthenware flagons. "You can't bring that in here," he said pointing at Boris, and jerking a thick thumb at the sign which hung over the bar behind him. "Timmy won't allow it."

"No magic, no animals, and no weapons," read Willow.

"We'll see about that!" said Granny, rapping her knuckles on the oak bar to attract the attention of the thick set barman with his back to us. "Service please! This moment!"

The man turned slowly and smiled. Barney took a step backwards, pulling me with him, his fingers digging into my wrist. "What the heck is that?" he said. "What on earth?"

"I could say the same about you," said the barman, scowling at Barney. "You're a little freakish yourself — you're taller than a horse, and we don't see many gingers in these parts. It's said that ginger hair indicates a soul of blackness, but I'm willing to judge a person on the merits of his or her character.

But to answer your insensitive question — I'm Timmy, and I'm unapologetically a troll."

Boris tapped Granny on her foot. "Urm," he said, gazing up at her. "I'm a goat and that's a troll. In the stories my mother used to read to me, there was always a little friction between the two, with goats usually coming off the worse. Far worse."

"Relax, little goat," said Timmy, peering over the bar, his voice far gentler than the mouth of sharp teeth, and narrow yellow eyes set deep in a twisted green tinged face, would have suggested. "I won't eat you. I will ask the people you're with why they thought it acceptable to bring an animal into my tavern, though. Can't any of you read?"

"I've read your sign," said Granny. "And I find it to be highly problematic. Since when did it become acceptable to discriminate based on gender, body weight or shape, IQ, culture, religion, physical ability, age, sexual preference, race, or in this despicable instance — species? I'll have you know that I've spent many years of my life fighting against social injustice, in and out of The Haven, and I will not tolerate your bigoted attitude — especially since you're of a species which has experienced its own fair share of discrimination over the centuries. You should be ashamed, sir! Ashamed!" She folded her arms and gave Timmy the practiced glare which normally made people cower.

Timmy gave Granny a grin which exposed a second row of teeth set behind the first. "Don't you come in here spouting that nonsense, old lady. You —"

"Oh!" said Granny. "You can't help yourself can you, you crusty disgusting creature. How dare you comment on my appearance, *and* get it so very wrong. You will serve us all with a beer each, and you shall serve Boris — the goat you've insulted, with some of your finest brandy, and we'd like it on the house, or my wrath will be swift and decisive!"

The troll gave a low laugh, and his eyes glowed a brighter yellow. "Crispin! Tarquin! Come here please!"

"Granny," said Willow. "Be careful."

From a door behind the bar appeared two hulking shapes, both of them with eyes as yellow as Timmy's, but with considerably wider shoulders and thicker necks. "Yes, boss?" said the tallest of the troll pair.

"Time to earn your money, boys," said Timmy. "We've got trouble makers in the tavern. The angry one with blue hair and purple glasses has threatened me with swift and decisive wrath if I don't let her goat stay and give them all a free drink."

"Go on then," said one of the bouncers, staring at Granny down a recently broken nose as he adjusted his long black coat. "Show us your wrath."

The music stopped and I became aware that

everyone in the room had stopped talking to train their eyes on us.

Granny looked slowly around the room and took a deep breath. "Okay," she whispered, reaching into a pocket.

CHAPTER NINE

"*L*et me see those hands!" said one of the bouncers.

"Relax," said Granny, retrieving the pouch of coins Maeve had given her. "It's just a money pouch, and I'm hoping it will buy me out of the unfortunate incident I've found myself embroiled in."

"What are you talking about?" said Timmy. "Where's the wrath you promised? My boys are dying to release some of their pent-up energy. It's been a little quiet in here recently. We could do with seeing a few people being tossed out of the door."

The two bouncer trolls grunted their agreement, and Granny put her hand on the largest one's arm. "Calm down, beefy," she said. "You won't be doing any tossing tonight. I find myself in a bit of a predicament. You see — nobody has ever stood up to me when I've threatened them with my wrath, but it seems you fellas are made of sterner stuff than the normal folk I cross words with. Add to that the fact that I'm suffering from a severe case of witch dementia, and it becomes clear that my threats were nothing more than crassness and bluster. For that, I apologise, and I'd like to offer you each a shiny gold coin in way of recompense, and to buy my companion Boris, the goat at the centre of this misunderstanding, his rightful place in your fine establishment."

Timmy laughed. "We don't need your gold!"

The shorter bouncer cleared his throat. "I could do with a little extra gold, boss," he said. "Jemima's going to give birth soon. She's expecting a large litter this time round, and us trolls don't have the privilege of being able to magic up food. Between this job and the new building job, I hardly earn enough to keep a roof over our heads. That gold would keep us fed for a month."

"I feel the same as Tarquin," grunted the other bouncer. "I need a new pair of boots. I dropped a metal sheet on my foot today and it went right through. My toe hurts, boss. I could use that gold."

Timmy rolled his eyes, the thick wrinkles in his forehead creaking like a leather jacket being folded.

"That'll teach you for working in the depths then, won't it? I told you it wasn't safe down there, and I don't trust the man you're working for. He's sly."

Granny rolled a coin between finger and thumb. "Come on, Timmy," she teased. "You know you want it. You trolls love hoarding wealth, and one of these gold pieces is worth more than a hundred flagons of your beer."

"Gladys," said Barney, smiling nervously at the trolls. "Why don't we just leave? It would be cheaper and simpler. I'm sure we can find a tavern that will allow Boris inside."

"Principle, dear boy," said Granny. "Boris has as much right to be here as everyone else in this room, and I want to prove to the management that he won't cause any problems. I can't leave here knowing that the next enchanted animal that walks into this tavern will be given the same treatment as Boris has received. I like to make positive changes wherever I go, and if it takes handing over money to achieve that change, then so be it. Plus, it's not really my money, is it? If Maeve is silly enough to hand over a bulging purse of coins to *me*, then she should know that some of it will be squandered foolishly. It's only right and proper."

Timmy sighed, the sickly aroma of pickled some-thing — possibly eggs, rolling across the bar in a gross invisible mist. "We'll take your gold, but that won't be enough." He nodded towards the corner where the band sat in nervous silence. "Tonight is open stage night. If any member of your group has a talent which will keep my customers entertained for a few minutes, then you're welcome to stay. If not, I'll take the gold anyway and *still* get the boys to toss you out."

"Thanks, boss," said Crispin. "You're a kind troll. Always thinking of others."

"Too kind sometimes," muttered Timmy. He ran his eyes over us. "Now, can any of you perform, or are my lads going to show you the door?"

"This is your chance, Boris!" said Granny. "Your chance to show these people, and trolls, that animals are not all dumb beasts of the field." She lay a hand on the goat's head. "Dance for us, Boris! The band will play a lively tune, and you can dance a lively jig! Bend those limbs and move that head, and wow us like you wowed the crowds at the animal show. I regret not being there to witness your moves that day, my dancing, prancing, sure-footed friend. But you can show me now! Get on stage and dance like you've never danced before!"

Boris looked at me and Willow for support.

"You've got the moves," said Willow.

"You did dance well at the show," I admitted,

"and it seemed like you had fun at the time. Not to mention the trophy you won. It's still got pride of place on Granny's mantelpiece. You must have been proud of your performance."

It had been almost eight weeks since Boris had won the Wickford and Covenhill best farm animal contest. His win had been clinched by the pirouette he'd performed at the judge's table, which had surprised Susie, Willow and I as much as it had surprised the judges and spectators. There had been just one small difference on that day, though. Boris had been extremely drunk. He still had alcohol in his veins from the brandy he'd drank at Maeve's house, but he was nowhere near as drunk as he'd been on the day of his victory.

"I *was* proud, Penny," said Boris. "It was a fine day."

"Have a brandy or two," I suggested. "Then dance." I looked at Timmy. "I'm sure the barman won't mind serving you a brandy if it means he can watch a dancing goat."

Timmy bit the gold piece Granny had handed him. "The gold's good," he said. "I suppose I can give the animal a few brandies — but be warned, if he fails to please the audience, you're all getting thrown out."

A man in the crowd shouted. "Get on with it! We want a show!"

Timmy took a large bottle of brandy from a shelf and handed it to Granny. "Satisfy your goat's thirst, but go easy — that brandy doesn't come cheap."

Granny tugged at the cork, removing it with a pop. "Open wide," she said, tilting the bottle towards Boris. "Take your fun juice."

Boris suckled at the bottle like a piglet at a teat, his throat contracting as he swallowed the amber liquid.

"That's enough!" said Timmy. "And wipe that bottle before you hand it back to me. That animal's teeth are disgusting!"

"You're a fine one to talk," said Granny, wiping the bottle rim on her sleeve and replacing the cork. She placed the brandy on the bar next to Timmy's muscled arm. "Was that enough, Boris? Have you lost your inhibitions yet?"

"Almost," said Boris. "I'll need to hear some music to help release my inner dancing beast."

Timmy clapped. "You heard him," he said, speaking to the band. "Play!"

One of the guitarists struck a melancholy chord, and the accordion player dragged out a long vibrating note. Boris shook his head, drops of brandy dripping from his beard. "No, no, no," he said. "That won't do! This ain't no funeral — this is a party!" He hurried to the stage and clambered up the two low steps, joining the confused band. He looked out over the crowd. "Any beatboxers in da house?" he shouted.

"I'll beat you into a wooden box and bury you alive in it if you don't hurry up and dance!" shouted Timmy, to loud guffaws from the crowd.

"What's a beatboxer?" called a woman from the back of the room.

"It's somebody who wants to be a musician, but hasn't got the self-discipline or skill to teach themselves to play a musical instrument," said Granny, raising her voice. "I know it sounds strange in this world, but imagine somebody invited you to dinner and using magic to prepare it instead of cooking it themselves. It's very, very lazy. A little like when my daughter tries to trick me into thinking she's cooked a curry, but I find the empty glass korma jars at the bottom of her bin, underneath the family sized chocolate bar wrappers, that she *apparently* doesn't eat anymore. Although her increasing clothing size tells a different story. A very different story indeed."

"Have you been going through my bins again, Mother?" said Mum. "I've told you before, you won't find any evidence of drug use in there. I like dancing naked to Lionel Richie music because it feels liberating — not because I'm stoned, and if you didn't keep spying on me on a Sunday morning, you wouldn't have to witness it!"

The cottages Mum and Granny lived in were each built on the peak of a hill — one at either extremity of Wickford. With a valley between them, the two women had long been spying on each other, with Mum utilising a high-powered telescope, and Granny using binoculars. The last I'd heard, they'd come to a truce, but it seemed Granny wasn't honouring it.

"Somebody has to look out for you, sweetheart," said Granny. "You're your own worst enemy."

"Erm, I can do a little," said Barney.

"A little what?" said Granny. "What are you talking about now, young man?"

"Beatboxing," said Barney. "I was into the hip-hop scene at school for a few months. I'm sure I could still knock out some killer beats."

"Well don't just stand there boasting," snapped Granny. "Get up on stage with that brave goat and drop some sounds."

I gave Barney a nervous smile. "School was a long time ago," I reminded him.

He took a deep breath. "I still practice now and again, it helps me bond with some of the young street gangs in Wickford. I call it cultural policing. You'd be surprised how easy it is to diffuse a crisis with a little mouth bass. I once stopped a potential blood bath between the Bus Stop Massive and the Duck Pond Posse by spitting chords. Young Charlie Wilkinson, leader of the BSM, had ripped the name tag out of Freddy Simpon's — leader of the DPP's, school gym shorts. The teacher had already punished Charlie by not allowing him to play football at lunch time, but Charlie was having none of it. He wanted blood, so I bought them both an ice cream and knocked out a few ghetto beats. Problem solved. Freddy went to Charlie's for a sleepover a week later, and now the two gangs have joined forces against the Playground Proud Boys."

His beaming smile told me he wasn't joking, and I put a gentle hand on his arm, pushing him in the direction of the stage. "I'm sure you'll do great," I said, ignoring Granny's snorting laughter.

"Go, Barney!" said Willow. "Show them what you can do!"

Barney climbed onto the stage and stood next to Boris, cupping a hand over his mouth. He began rocking from foot to foot, his long legs gaining a little rhythm as he made a repetitive deep bass drum sound, interspersed by higher pitched sounds which reminded me of the laser weapons used in Star Trek. His lips vibrated and his mouth opened and closed, and Boris's rear end swayed in time to the sounds as Barney increased the tempo.

Boris turned to the band. "Play!" he said. "In time with the beat-meister!"

The guitarists looked at one another, and with

their feet tapping in time to Barney's sounds, began playing rhythmic chords. The accordion player joined in, playing low notes and nodding his head to the beat. When the singer joined in, her voice complimenting Barney's beatboxing perfectly, even my foot tapped to the beat, and a smile slid over my face.

A loud whistle from somebody in the crowd and a round of applause spurred the band on, and Boris began shaking his whole body, his head nodding faster and faster as the band played louder. People began thumping the wooden tables with their flagons, in time to the beat, and Boris threw himself into the air, his legs making a star shape and his spine arched in a curve.

"What's he doing?" shouted Timmy, as Boris crashed into the stage and began writhing like a dying fish. "Is he possessed by a demon? Should I call an exorcist?"

"It's called the caterpillar," I said. "He's performing what we call break-dancing."

Boris threw himself onto his back and the crowd roared their appreciation as he began spinning, his legs drawn close to his body and his chin close to his chest.

"He'll break his legs if he's not careful," said Timmy, his hand tapping out the beat on the bar. "They're too spindly for that sort of exertion."

Boris leapt to his feet as Barney rocked from side

to side, beatboxing with obvious enthusiasm and pulling his shorts down a few inches to expose the elasticated band of his red underwear.

"Is he a stripper too?" shouted a woman. "I hope so. It's been too long since I saw a gentleman's ding-a-ling. My Harold's been at the pies a little too much lately. His belly gets in the way."

"No! He's *not* a stripper," I shouted. "Some people in our world who enjoy this sort of music wear their trousers like that. It's a fashion statement."

"It's a blight on humanity," said Granny. "Gone are the days of the Rockers and Teddy boys. Now those young cats dressed with dignity, not like narrow waisted ruffians."

As the music got faster and Boris slid seamlessly into the move I knew as crazy-legs, Crispin stepped from behind the bar and approached me. The huge troll strutted toward me in time with the music and reached for my hand, gripping it in his shovel sized palm and tugging me toward him. "Dance with me, female!" he demanded.

I pulled my hand from his and stepped backwards. "That's not how you speak to a lady," I said. "I'm sure you're a hit with the girls, aren't you?"

"That's how we trolls show our affection for the weaker sex," said Crispin. "The lady trolls love it."

"Weaker sex?" said Granny. "How dare you! You misogynistic animal! When I get my magic back I'm going to pay this tavern another visit and cast a spell on you — so powerful that your kidneys will pop out of your ears! Now step away from my granddaughter and thank your lucky stars that my magic is not accessible now."

"Stop the music!" shouted Timmy, his roaring voice scaring the band into silence and stopping Boris mid moonwalk. "I've had enough. You troublemakers should leave now."

Mum tapped me on my shoulder and passed me her handkerchief. "Wipe your hand, darling," she said. "You've got some sort of disgusting troll bodily fluid on it."

I took the handkerchief and looked at my hand. It was dark with a dusty deposit which stained my fingers.

"That's not bodily fluid!" said Crispin. "That's the dust from an honest hard day's work in the depths. That's what that is!"

The white handkerchief darkened as I rubbed my hand clean. Barney joined me, pulling his trousers up and wiping an accumulation of spittle from his chin. "Beatboxing is a messy business," he said. "Let me use that hanky after you."

He took the dirty piece of linen and studied it for a second. "This looks familiar," he said, examining the stains. "My granddad was a roofer and his white t-shirt looked like this when he'd been working with lead and wiped his hands clean on it. I'm no Sherlock Holmes, but I know a clue when I see one." He looked at Crispin. "Why do you have lead dust on your hands?"

Crispin frowned. "From working in the depths. I already told the female. It's the dust from the same metal that almost took a toe off my foot when I dropped a sheet of it on my boot."

"What work?" said Barney. "And what are the depths?"

"We're building a —"

"Quiet!" said Quentin, putting a huge hand on his fellow bouncer's shoulder. "Stay your wagging tongue and say no more! The man we work for told us to speak to nobody of our work, and there's something about him which tells me he should not be crossed."

"It's important," said Barney. "We're looking for —"

"Enough!" shouted Timmy. "This isn't an establishment in which people gossip to strangers. This isn't Twiggy's General Store and Tattoo Parlour! The people who sit in her chair to be decorated may be liberal with their tongues, but secrets spoken in The Nest of Vipers stay within these walls. Now be gone — I'm itching to see if that goat can fly as well as he dances, and my boys are itching to be the trolls who launch him."

Knowing we'd more than outstayed our welcome, we left the tavern quickly, with Granny reiterating her threat that she'd return when her magic was back.

Willow led the way to the boat, her spell leading her quickly along side streets and through narrow alleyways until the harbour opened up before us. The Water Witch's bright red and green paintwork shone in the yellow light emitted from the street-lamps, and distant sounds of people having fun bounced across the water's surface.

Boris stopped as we approached the boat, his head cocked to the side and his ears twitching. "Something is wrong," he said. "I can hear footsteps on the boat. Somebody's aboard the Water Witch!"

Barney broke into a run, shouting at us to stay back. His warning to us served as a warning to whoever was on the boat too, and with a thumping sound on wooden steps and a slam of the bow decking door, the dark shape of somebody wearing a flowing cloak appeared on the Water Witch and glanced in our direction.

Barney approached the gangplank at speed, almost slipping on the damp stone surface of the dockside, but regaining his balance as the intruder lifted an arm in our direction. "Stop right there!" shouted Barney. "Stay where you are!"

The intruder stood still and gave a low laugh.

"It's a man," said Granny, as the intruder laughed again.

Barney reached the gangplank just as the man lifted his arm and emitted a shower of colourful sparks from his fingertips. The buzz of electric in the air accompanied the light show, and Barney let out a cry of pain as he was thrown backwards through the air, his arms flailing and his head thudding on stone as he slammed into the hard floor.

"Barney!" I yelled, as the man climbed over the bow railings on the water side of the boat.

"He's jumped in the river!" said Mum.

The thud of feet on wood disproved Mum, and as I arrived at Barney's side and cradled his head in my hands, the roar of an engine starting drowned out Barney's groans.

"He's on a boat!" said Granny.

The long hull of the Water Witch had afforded the stranger's boat a perfect hiding place, but as it slid into view with the man at the controls, it was obvious even in the darkness that the hull was painted a vivid red.

"I'll stop him," said Mum, magic sparking at her fingertips. The spell left her hand at speed, the golden stream of light flying straight and true until it neared the boat where it spread over the hull in an umbrella shape, before fizzing and spluttering out of existence.

"A forcefield," said Granny. "It's powerful magic."

Barney groaned again, and I watched helplessly as the boat slid into darkness. "Forget it," I said, as Willow and Boris hurried along the dockside in a pointless attempt at following the stranger. "Help me with Barney. I can't lift him on my own."

CHAPTER TEN

*B*arney took a bite of toast and sipped his tea. "Amazing," he said, rubbing his head for the umpteenth time since he'd woken up. "The lump has totally vanished and there's no pain at all."

"You can thank Penny for that," said Willow, tossing Rosie's stuffed toy mouse along the length of the boat. "Her healing spell is second to none."

Rosie chased the mouse through the boat and pounced on it as it landed next to Willow's bedroom door, giving a satisfied mewl and settling down to chew on her prey.

"Should we check again?" said Willow. "Surely he must have taken something. Why else would he break in?"

The intruder hadn't even damaged the door he'd used to gain entry to the boat through, using magic to unlock it rather than brute force, and if we hadn't arrived at the boat when we had, it was doubtful we'd have ever known somebody had been aboard. As far as we could tell, after an exhaustive search which went on into the early hours of the morning, nothing had been taken and nothing had been damaged. Mum had done a sweep of the boat checking for sleeper spells which may have been cast. She and Granny had explained that some spells could be cast and left to fizz away in the ether, unseen until they were triggered by the person who'd cast them. Mum had found nothing, and with the bright sunlight spilling in through the boat's windows, and music playing on the CD player, we all felt safer and more cheerful than we had the night before.

Barney buttered another piece of toast. "We're all in agreement that the person on the boat last night must be the person who's responsible for taking the witches, and we can safely assume that the boat he was on is the boat the dwarfs told us about."

"Agreed," I said. "And we can be equally sure that he's the same man the trolls are working for in the depths — whatever they are — and that lead has a big part to play in it all."

"And that the lead is being used to deflect magic," said Boris. "We're all in agreement on that front too."

"What?" said Willow. "When did we speak about that?"

"We didn't," said Boris. "Did we need to? Are you all telling me that it hadn't crossed your mind that lead works against magic in the same way it does against radiation in the mortal world? Why do you think magic can't be used in the Silver Mountains? Because of the lead, and I'd bet a bottle of the finest brandy that there are lead deposits in every part of The Haven where magic can't be used." He looked around the table. "Really? Nobody picked up on it? I assumed it didn't need saying as it was so blatantly obvious."

Granny gave Boris a pat on the head. "You forget that your Oxford education affords you a far greater intellect than the rest of us, Boris. Think of us as village simpletons and yourself as Einstein — the chasm between our intelligence levels is that glaringly wide. I'm so proud of you."

"I thought of it," mumbled Barney.

"You did?" said Granny. "So why didn't you mention it?"

"I wrote it in my notebook."

Granny held out a hand, tapping the palm with a finger. "Let me see."

"It's in my other shorts," said Barney.

"I'll get them," said Granny. "Where are they."

"Okay, I put my hands up," said Barney. "I didn't think of it, but I would have got there eventually. I have a process, and I trust that process."

"Well put some more fuel in the process's tank," said Granny. "It's running on fumes at the moment."

Barney pushed his plate away and stood up. "Excuse me," he said. "I'm going to take a shower."

I waited for Barney to enter the small bathroom and close the door behind himself before I narrowed my eyes and stared at Granny. "It was Barney who realised it was lead on the handkerchief last night," I said. "And it was Barney who ran towards danger when we found somebody on the boat. I think we're doing well as a *team*, and anyway, Granny — what has your contribution been towards the solving of the mystery? All you've done is get stoned and cause an argument with trolls."

"I've got other problems too," said Granny. "I can't be using all of my grey matter on the problem of the missing witches, I've got to save some brain power for coming up with a way to split my sister and Derek up. There is absolutely no way that that pair are ever becoming an *item*. So, forgive me if I haven't *contributed* to solving the mystery *just* yet. I'm sure my time will come, and I'm equally sure that when it does I will shine. Brighter than you lot. That's for sure." She gave Boris another gentle pat on the head. "Not you of course. Nobody can shine brighter than you, Boris."

"The gesture is appreciated, Gladys," said Boris, getting to his feet, "but undeserved. We all deserve praise, and we all shine in different ways. I consider myself lucky to be able to call you all friends. Now, as it seems you three have bickering to carry on with, I'm going to take a leaf from Barney's book and leave you to it. I fancy a walk along the waterfront. I need a breath of fresh air and some time to think."

"Don't go too near the edge of the river," shouted Granny, as Boris climbed the steps up to the decking. "And don't go speaking to strangers!"

"I won't," came the distant reply.

"I'd prefer it if you didn't speak to me in that way in front of Boris," said Granny, glaring at me. "Asking me what my contribution to solving the crime has been — you made me look silly."

"Oh, stop worrying what that goat thinks about you," said Mum. "You act around him like you used to act around Dad. You're like an old married couple, and it's embarrassing!"

"How dare you call my relationship with Boris embarrassing," said Granny. Sparks rolled from her fingertips and her eyes glazed over.

"Careful, Granny," said Willow. "Dementia, remember. Don't do anything you'll regret."

Granny watched the sparks at her fingers and took a deep breath. The sparks vanished as quickly as Granny's mood shifted from angry to upset. "Why is everything so difficult?" she said, a tear forming in her eye. "Why did I have to get witch dementia? It's not like it runs in our family. It's my dementia's fault that Charleston is trapped in the body of a goat!"

"Well take the damned dementia cure for goodness sake!" said Mum. "What's wrong with you? It's a simple fix!"

Granny seemed not to have heard Mum. "And it's my dementia's fault that I've fallen in lov —" She stopped speaking and put a hand to her mouth, as if to stop anymore words tumbling out, and her body shook as she sobbed.

"What did you say?" said Mum.

"Don't, Mum," I said, putting an arm around Granny. "She's upset."

"Oh, Penny," gasped Granny, pushing her head tight against my chest. "I've got a secret that will make you all hate me if I reveal it."

"What secret?" said Willow. "Are you okay, Granny? What's wrong?"

Granny seemed to have shrunk in my arms, and her bony shoulder dug into my flesh. I put a hand on her head, and pulled her tighter to me. "It's okay, Granny," I said. "I know your secret, and so does Barney. You told us after smoking the pipe of peace, and Barney and I don't hate you. We love you."

"I told you?" she said, looking up at me through teary eyes. "And you don't hate me?"

"You did," I said, squeezing her tight. "And of course I don't."

"It had to come out at some point," she said, hiding her face in my bosom. "I couldn't hide it forever! It's been burning a hole in my very soul! What would Norman, rest his soul, think? He'll be spinning in his grave knowing he had a harlot for a wife!"

"Mother?" said Mum, her voice soft. "What's going on?"

"I'm worried," said Willow. "Granny, you know we love you. You can tell us anything."

"Anything," said Mum.

Granny looked up, her cheeks puffy and her eyes bloodshot. "Anything?" she sobbed. "Even that I've fallen in love with another man and betrayed your grandfather, Willow?" She turned her gaze to Mum. "I can tell you that I've betrayed your father, Maggie? Because that's what I've done. I've gone and fallen in love with a Chinese acupuncturist. I've gone and fallen in love with Charleston, and when I take my dementia cure I'll lose him. I can't tell him of course, he harbours no romantic feelings towards me. Why would he?" She wiped her cheeks with a shaking hand, and stared up at me. "What would Norman, rest his soul, think? It's a saving grace that Charleston is Chinese and not Japanese. Norman, rest his soul, loved Chinese food, but hated what the Japanese did in Pearl Harbour. That's the only positive I can draw from this terrible mess!"

"The only positive you can draw from all this is that Granddad was a little racist?" I said. "What about the fact that you've fallen in love? That's a beautiful positive."

"Mother," said Mum. "We're not the sort of family who judges one another in matters of the heart. We never have been. I loved Dad, yes, but I love you too. I want you to be happy."

"I'm sure Granddad would too," said Willow. "He's probably looking down on you, happy that you're happy."

"What?" said Granny. "Your grandfather once made a man cry because I commented on how nice his suit was. Norman, rest his soul, was a jealous man, a very jealous man indeed. He won't be smiling down on me, he'll be bubbling with rage. I can picture him now, his right eyebrow arched and his knuckle duster ready for action."

"Knuckle duster?" said Willow. "Granddad?"

"Oh yes," said Mum. "You'd be surprised, Willow."

"How else do you think he made a grown man cry?" said Granny. "He wasn't big or strong, he needed back up for the occasions on which his mouth wrote cheques that his body couldn't cash."

"You can't base your future life on what Dad was like," said Mum. "That was the past. Your future is your future, and if you want my advice, you'd tell

Boris, I mean Charleston, how you feel about him. You might be surprised. He speaks of you in very high regard, and I think I speak for everyone else when I say that we're all very fond of him too."

Willow and I nodded our agreement, and Granny gave Mum an affectionate smile. "You fatties are always very optimistic," she said, resting her hand on Mum's. "Maybe it's the raised cholesterol playing havoc with the thought process, I don't know, but I admire your outlook, Maggie. On this occasion, I think your optimism is misplaced, though. Charleston won't look twice at me when he's back in his real body. He'll be gone from my guest bedroom the second his body is no longer frozen by magic. That room will be empty without him. I like to go in there sometimes to comb his hair and polish his ring. It's got a lovely stone in it – a *real* diamond, I think."

The bathroom door opened, spewing a cloud of steam into the boat. "That's better," said Barney, emerging from the mist. "There's nothing like a hot shower to get the blood pumping."

Granny sat up straight and wiped her eyes with a paper towel. "Not a word to anyone else about what just happened at this table," she hissed.

"Barney knows," I reminded her.

"He doesn't know that *I know* he knows," whispered Granny. "And I want it to remain that way. This is woman talk. I won't discuss emotions with a man

134

— it makes them flighty and hungry. That's why men with over emotional wives tend to be anxious and fat. It's not fair on them. Men aren't built to speak about love as openly as us women."

The sound of hooves thudding on the decking put a stop to anymore conversation concerning Granny's love life, and Granny wiped the final tear from her cheek as Boris pushed past Barney and stood next to the table. "I've found the shop that the trolls mentioned last night," he said. "Twiggy's General Store and Tattoo Parlour. It's just around the corner. Shall we go? If Twiggy is as much of a gossip as the trolls made out, then you never know what she might be able to tell us."

"Clever goat!" said Granny. "Let's get going, right this moment. We've got a mystery to solve! There are six witches out there who need our help. Time is of the essence!"

CHAPTER ELEVEN

Two hours and twenty minutes later, we all stood outside the shop. Granny had wasted an hour insisting on finding the hairbrush she'd misplaced, finally admitting reluctantly that she may not have brought it with her, and even more reluctantly using Mum's brush instead, pulling handfuls of black hairs from the bristles before taking the risk of running it through her blue hair. The second hour had been taken up by carefully removing tiny splinters of wood from Rosie's gums. She'd discovered a small twig in Willow's bedroom while searching for her stuffed mouse, and had chewed it into a yellow mush which Willow scooped up with a paper towel and tossed in the bin.

The final twenty minutes had been spent strolling

along the waterfront, taking in the atmosphere of the city by day, and looking out for the red boat we'd seen the night before. Mum had cast a spell over the Water Witch before we'd left, making it impossible for anyone to get within a foot of the hull. If the man on the red boat did return, he'd have no luck if he tried illegally boarding my boat again.

Twiggy's General Store and Tattoo Parlour stood on a corner, the open door spewing the tantalising aromas of spices and herbs which mingled with the yeasty smell of fresh baked bread. The term *General Store* seemed a little tame as we stepped inside. Twiggy's seemed to stock everything — more a universal store than a general store. Shelves brimming with huge ripe melons sat opposite shelves crammed with thick woolly sweaters, and a glass cabinet placed next to a rack full of wine bottles was filled with magic wands of various lengths and aesthetic appeal.

A huge oven stood near the doorway, and I watched fascinated as a man dressed in traditional baker's clothing withdrew a large brown loaf, using a long wooden paddle to retrieve it from the hot interior. Women and men browsed the aisles, and children gathered around a stand displaying hand carved wooden puppets — some of them painted and dressed as clowns and others as witches and wizards. One child had removed a particularly colourful clown from the stand, and with expert control of the strings, was making it dance, much to the delight of the other children. The whole shop smelt delicious, and I had already decided that the evening meal was going to consist of one of the fat honey roast hams which stood on the meat counter, accompanied by a few of the soil covered freshly harvested new potatoes which filled a wooden barrel.

Barney pointed towards the rear of the shop. "That's where we should be," he said. "The trolls said people gossip while they get tattoos."

Twiggy's Tattoos, read the sign hanging from the ceiling, painted with an arrow which pointed to a staircase leading to the upper floor. The staircase creaked as we trudged up it and took a turn to the right near the top before opening into a spacious room, the high walls adorned with tattoo designs and fantastical paintings of dragons, and other strange creatures, which I hoped were mythical and not accurate representations of haven residents.

Old leather sofas and chairs provided seating for customers awaiting a tattoo, and a single seat beneath a bright light was the chair in which customers were inked. Nobody was waiting, but a huge man with a bare chest and full beard was currently being worked on by a tall woman with a body that ran straight up and down, with no discernible bumps or curves beneath the green velvet body hugging dress she wore. "No prizes for guessing that she's Twiggy," I said under my breath.

Twiggy leaned over the man in the chair, and with a wand in hand, made shapes in the air a few inches above his bulging pectoral muscle. "Wow," said Boris. "No needles."

Colours and shapes appeared on the customer's sun browned skin as the wand danced through the air, and as I approached the chair for a better look, the shapes shifted on the man's skin. The tattoo was of a ship, but what was remarkable was the way the vessel rode the incandescent blue waves which Twiggy was working on. The galleon dipped into deep troughs of water and rode the peaks of tall waves, tilting from side to side as it ploughed through the rough sea, going nowhere on the man's chest.

"That's amazing," I said, standing behind Twiggy. "Do you mind if I watch?"

"I don't mind," said the tall woman, her eyes resting on me briefly. "Do you mind, Jimmy?" she asked, returning her attention to the magical tattoo she was creating.

The big man smiled at me. "Watch all you want," he said. "You thinking of having one?"

"No, she is not!" said Mum, standing beside me.

"I'll have one if I want, Mum," I said. "But I

don't think I'm ready for one just yet. If I ever get one I want it to mean something special."

"Like this one," said the big man, tapping his chest with a wide finger. "The ship you're looking at is the galleon that I took my last voyage aboard. It went down with all hands lost apart from me. I was lucky. It happened in the mortal world and I'd already been given my haven entry spell. The ship was completely underwater and sinking fast when I manged to open a portal in the captain's cabin doorway. I was almost out of air when I swam through. The other poor souls had no chance."

Twiggy made a final mark on the man's skin, adding a sailor to the crow's nest at the tip of the tallest mast. "There," she said. "All done."

I moved nearer to the man's chest for a better look. The sailor in the tattoo was small, but the thick beard which blew in a non-existent breeze gave away his identity. "That's you, isn't it?" I said, resisting the urge to touch the tattoo as the ship dipped and rose on the man's chest — going nowhere, but giving the illusion it was moving at speed through the swelling ocean.

"Aye," said the man. "That's me. I was on lookout duty. I never saw the iceberg that broke the bow, and I'll never forgive myself either. This tattoo is a reminder of how I failed all those men I sailed with."

Mum drew a sharp intake of breath as an iceberg

floated into view in the path of the boat. I was almost convinced that I heard the splintering of wood as the boat was torn apart by the sharp ice and began sinking, the broken bow sliding quickly beneath the surface. The man drew his shirt over his tattoo. "There's no need for you good ladies to see the worse part. That's my penance. Each time I look in a mirror I'll be reminded of the people I let down that day."

Twiggy put a hand on the man's shoulder. "Try to forgive yourself, Jimmy, and when you do, come back so I can remove it. You'll be alive a long time in The Haven, and having that reminder on your chest will do no good for your soul. It'll send you mad."

Jimmy smiled and handed Twiggy some coins. "I don't want to forgive myself," he said. "I want to remember. It keeps those men alive in my heart."

Twiggy and Jimmy hugged, and when the large man had left, Twiggy looked around the room. "Who's next?" she said, with a smile. "The goat? I've never tattooed an animal before, it could be fun."

"I'm sorry," I said. "We're not here for tattoos. We were hoping you could help us. We're looking for six witches who have gone missing."

Twiggy looked down at me, her thin neck decorated in swirls of black ink, and her eyes piercing and thoughtful. "How do you think I can help?" she said. "I know nothing of the missing witches. I've heard

141

about them, of course, but I don't think I can be of help to you people — whoever you are."

Barney joined us and stood at my side. He withdrew his notebook and looked at Twiggy. "We're just people who want to help," he said. "Would you consider answering some questions?"

"I don't know where you come from," said Twiggy. "But nobody likes a loose tongue in the City of Shadows. They don't tend to stay in the mouth for long, and I'm quite attached to mine. I'm sorry, but you'll be getting no help from me."

Barney glanced at his notes. "It really would help," he said. "Just a few simple questions."

Twiggy ignored Barney and stared over my shoulder. "Who's that woman?" she said. "The one sneaking down the stairs. The one who hasn't turned to face me since she came in here and saw me? The one with blue hair. I know her. I'd recognise that plump bottom anywhere. I recognise all the flesh and bone canvases I've worked on." She took a few steps towards Granny. "It's you, isn't it... Gladys...Weaver?"

Granny paused on the third step down. "My name is not Gladys," she said without turning around, her voice a few octaves higher than usual. She took another step. "I am a simple woman. My name is... erm, my name is.... John Jones. No! Joanne Jones, my name is Joanne Jones and I am but a simple washer woman who wandered into your place of business by accident. Please forgive me, I should be going now. I have washing to... wash."

"I'd know you anywhere, Gladys," said Twiggy, crossing the room. "Why do you hide from me? Do you not remember me? We spent time in prison together. I tattooed your right buttock using a sewing needle and the red ink you stole from the warden's office. Of course it's you, Gladys — I'd never forget the person I created my first ever tattoo on."

"You have a tattoo, Gladys?" said Boris. "How exciting."

"I'm not Gladys," said Granny, her shoulders slumping.

"The game's up, Granny, come on," said Willow. "And what's she talking about... tattoos and prison? We knew you'd spent an hour or two in the Wickford police cells in the past, but you've never mentioned prison!"

"We spent a terrible time together in prison," said Twiggy, holding a hand to her chest as if to calm herself. "Here in The Haven. We shared a cell, and during our incarceration we became blood sisters, cutting our flesh and mixing our lifelines with the promise that we'd always be there for one another." She took a step closer to Granny. "Why do you hide your face from me now, Gladys? Does our pact no longer stand? Are we no longer sisters of blood? I tattooed you, Gladys, you bare my artwork on your fleshy behind, surely that still means something to you?"

Granny turned to face Twiggy. "Of course it means something," she said, her eyes shimmering with tears. "I didn't want my family to know my shame, that's all, and I certainly didn't want them to know I wear a tattoo. I'd have never come in your shop if I'd recognised the name, but you weren't known as Twiggy when we were held in that prison hell-hole, like rats in a trap."

"I took the name after leaving prison," Twiggy said. "I needed a change. I wanted to feel reborn when I felt the first breath of free air on my cheeks and the grass beneath my feet. Twiggy was the name my brother gave me when I was young, due to my build. I thought it fitted quite well."

"It fits beautifully," said Granny, climbing the stairs and approaching her old friend. "Illyria never really rolled off the tongue. Twiggy is simpler."

"Tattoo?" I said, staring at Granny. "What tattoo do you have on your arse, Granny?"

"It's nothing," said Granny. "Forget it was ever mentioned."

Twiggy gasped. "Nothing! How can you say that? It meant so much to you back then!" She looked at me, her eyes twinkling. "Its meaning was lost on me of course — I left the mortal world centuries ago and never kept up with developments, but your grandmother assured me that one day the symbol and slogan I inked on her derriere would be known throughout your world, and worshipped by all." Twiggy smiled at Granny. "Did it happen, Gladys Weaver? Did the red-heaven you spoke and sang of come true? Is your world a place of equality and peace as you predicted it would be?"

Granny looked at the floor. "Not quite," she said.

"What's the tattoo?" said Willow.

"It was beautiful," said Twiggy. "It was never my best work of art, of course, but it was my first, and the fact it was a prison tattoo made it so much more special. It was a simple design, but with great meaning to your dear grandmother. I can see it now, a crossed hammer and sickle, above the slogan — Rise, Comrades! The cleverest part was the phrase above it though, wasn't it, Gladys?"

Granny grunted.

"Unroot evil, it reads," said Twiggy. "An anagram of revolution! Beautiful."

Granny blushed. "It was a long time ago. My politics have changed a little since that time."

"I think it comes as no surprise to most of us that you lean very much to the left, Gladys," said Boris. "Maybe just a tad *too* far on some occasions, but it seems the revelation that you were incarcerated in a haven prison is news to your family. What did you do, Gladys? What crime did you commit?"

"What crime did *we* commit?" said Twiggy, laying a hand of solidarity on Granny's shoulder. "Gladys was the founder and leader of our movement — the Social Justice Witches. We made great changes in The Haven, until one night we were betrayed." She lowered her eyes. "Betrayed by one of our own."

"Big Bertha," spat Granny, her fist clenched. "The big bitch."

"Yes," said Twiggy. "Big Bertha let it be known that we were planning an operation — *Gladys* was planning an operation, she was the mastermind behind all our actions after all. Gladys planned to disrupt a man only event, in protest against the patriarchy and their refusal to allow female participation. Sexist pigs!"

"What was the event?" said Barney.

"A competition," said Twiggy. "To see who could grow the fullest beard in two weeks without the use of magic. We never got close enough to the event to disrupt it though, did we, Gladys?"

"No," muttered Granny, a vein in her forehead pulsating with angry blood. "Big Bertha had given the game away. Derek and his cronies were waiting for us. They confiscated our scissors, eggs, and hair removal potions — and tossed us into prison without trial. That was the end of the SJW's. The prison system tore us apart as a group and broke us as individuals."

"It did," said Twiggy. "But here we stand, Gladys Weaver — reunited after all this time, and with a bond between us so strong that only people who've been prison inmates could ever hope to understand it."

"Good lord," said Mum, pulling Granny close to her in a fierce hug. "I never knew. You poor, poor woman. How long were you locked up for, and why did I never know? Was it before I was born? Did you try to shield me from the shame? You needn't have! I'd have understood!"

"Two nights and almost three long days," said Granny, her voice faltering. "The worst weekend of my life. You were fourteen years old. Your father told you I'd gone to visit cousin Beryl in Cleethorpes. He couldn't tell you that your mother was a lag. I wouldn't allow it!"

Granny stumbled as Mum pushed her away. "A weekend! A bloody weekend!"

"A long weekend," interjected Twiggy, "and they ran out of teabags on the Sunday. It was awful. It was inhumane!"

"You sang communist songs, became a blood sister, had a prison tattoo, *and* were broken by the system over a weekend?" I said. "It must have been some prison."

"It was terrible!" said Granny. "You'll never understand — not until your liberty is snatched from you by force!"

"Take comfort that I understand, Gladys," said Twiggy. "I know your pain, and as your blood sister I will do all I can to help you and your family." She turned to Barney. "Ask your questions. I will answer them."

CHAPTER TWELVE

*A*fter Granny had introduced us all to her old prison friend, Barney reeled off a series of questions. Twiggy looked around the room before answering, as if to search for eavesdroppers. "The depths," she said quietly. "I've heard talk of it. Some of the men who sit in my chair come from work dirty with dust from their labour, and speak of a place known as the depths."

"What is it?" said Granny. "I've never heard of it and I've been around The Haven a bit."

"It's said that The City of Shadows is built upon another city, a smaller city, a city that sank in swampland and was lost to time, a city that now hides beneath our feet... in the depths. The men who work there speak of it being discovered by a strange man who possesses great power. He employs people to

149

build for him, beneath our feet, but *what* they build…
I do not know."

"Do you know what the man looks like, and if he
has a boat?" said Barney. "A red boat to be specific."

"What I've told you is all I know," said Twiggy.
"If you'd like to know what despicable man is having
an affair with whose despicable wife, and where the
finest happy herb can be had for cheap, then I could
talk all day, but most of the people who sit in my
chair know when they've said too much. They seem
nervous of speaking of the depths and the man who
employs them. I do not push them for more. Until
today it's never been of great importance to me, but
now you tell me it may be connected with the missing
witches. Do you think they are down there? Trapped
in the depths, like Gladys and I were trapped in Sunny
Mountain Open Prison and Recreation Centre?"

"I think it's a *little* worse than that," I said. "They
could be in *real* danger. Can you tell us how to reach
the depths? Is there a doorway? A hidden tunnel?"

Twiggy shook her head. "I'm sorry," she said. "I
don't know. Though if I were to search for the depths
myself I'd begin at the lowest point of the city."

"The docks." said Barney. "The same level as
the river."

"No," said Twiggy. "There is a lower place.
Before the dock side walls were built higher, the river
used to be held back by magic when heavy rainfall

poured from the mountains. If it wasn't controlled, the flood water would find its way to the old part of the city, where the spire of light is built. It sits in a dip, at the edge of the city."

"Spire of light?" said Barney, adding more notes to his book. "What's that?"

Twiggy looked at Granny. "He's a lawman you say? You would think he would have more sense." She smiled at Barney in the way a teacher smiles at a child who can't grasp a simple concept. "It's a spire," she said. "With a light atop it… the spire of light."

Barney scribbled another note in his book, his eyes flickering with annoyance for a moment. The pages in his book were beginning to fill up with random notes, and I wondered just how close we were to being able to help Maeve solve her mystery and find the missing witches. It seemed that although we had some clues, the investigation — if we could call it that, was disjointed, almost like it needed a metaphorical lynch pin to hold it together. Finding the depths was of paramount importance.

Twiggy looked towards the stairs as heavy footsteps approached. A man appeared, glancing around at the artwork which covered the walls. "Have you got time to do a tattoo, Twiggy?" he said.

Twiggy gave us an apologetic smile. "I'm sorry, I can't help you any further — duty calls, but before you leave," she said, "please allow me to make you a

gift. Take what you will from the shop downstairs."
She handed Mum a metal token. "Take this — it will
tell my staff that it's free of charge. I had some fresh
eggs delivered this morning, laid without magic, and
my baker is working on a new bread recipe — spell
free of course, and using only the finest whole grains.
Take what you will." She pulled Granny into a
lingering hug. "And now you know where to find me,
Gladys, don't be a stranger. You are my blood sister
after all."

With Granny promising to return, we left Twiggy
with her customer and browsed the shelves downstairs. Deciding we didn't want to take advantage of
Twiggy's kind offer, we filled a single paper bag with
half a ham, a dozen eggs, and a loaf of warm bread. It
would make a lovely supper, and the Water Witch was
already stocked with the non-perishables we needed.
There was no need to be greedy.

The young girl behind the sales counter brimmed
with happy energy and with a smile, took the token
Twiggy had given us. "The ham is lovely," she said.
"You'll enjoy it, and the eggs are fresher than a
breeze from the northern sea."

Boris glanced behind the counter, his eyes on the
large metal safe which was bolted to the wall.
"What's in there?" he asked.

A sign was propped on top of the safe, the words
on it written in large red letters.

Please ask a member of staff if you wish to make a special purchase. This safe is locked with magic, and only Twiggy has the power to open it.

"The valuable things," said the girl. "We had a problem with thieves, so Twiggy was forced to use a safe."

"What sort of valuable things?" said Willow.

"Just the normal stuff," said the girl. "Jewels from the ice-caps of the north, love potions made by the elderly voodoo witches, and liquorice root."

"Liquorice root?" said Barney. "That's rare?"

"Very much so," said the girl, twirling a strand of curly brown hair around a finger. "It's very rare indeed. It only grows in one part of The Haven — The Ridge of The Morning Sun. Few people can grow it, and many people love it. Good liquorice can't be grown with magic, it spoils the delicate taste. It's used for making alcoholic drinks, and chewing. Having a tin full of liquorice root is a sign of high status indeed. It's only become available for sale in Twiggy's shop in recent months — since Twiggy formed a trading agreement with the dwarfs of the Silver Mountains. I do not know how they come by it — they live where no crops will grow and no farmed animals roam, but suddenly they have an abundance of fine spices and bags full of liquorice root. Twiggy asks them no questions, though, she's happy that she makes such a large profit. The dwarfs wont deal in

SAM SHORT

gold, so Twiggy pays them with meats, eggs, and grains."

"So, it would be unusual for a man to simply toss a liquorice root to a goat?" I said.

"Unless he was *very* attached to the animal, or was able to grow the root himself. It would be comparable to you tossing a diamond to someone in the mortal world. It would be unheard of, unless you owned a diamond mine or had taken leave of your senses."

CHAPTER THIRTEEN

*M*aeve gave me a stern glare, her eyes dancing with emotion — flickering between incredulity, hurt, and as her eyes bored into mine — anger. "Derek would do no such thing!" she said. "This is your grandmother's doing! She's always harboured hatred for Derek. She's put thoughts into your head!"

Heading straight back to the boat after leaving Twiggy's shop, and piecing together snippets of information as we walked, we'd summoned Maeve as soon as we had formed a viable explanation for why we suspected Derek of being involved in the disappearance of the witches. Maeve wasn't taking it well, convinced we had misinterpreted the information in Barney's notebook.

Granny sighed. "I've done no such thing."

"The story you summoned me to listen to is a wild one indeed," said Maeve. "I find it hard to believe. Derek has been loyal to me for centuries."

Granny took a hard-boiled egg from a dish and mashed it into a lumpy paste on a slice of buttered bread. A slice of ham topped off the open sandwich, and she chewed as she spoke. "My sister is with Derek!" she said. "Whether you like it or not, or think I'm biased, I happen to love Eva, and I want to know she's safe! Think about it, Maeve. Derek could easily be taking on the form of his younger self — a fine disguise, nobody would suspect he was as handsome as he was in the portrait hanging in your house. Everyone thinks of him as a tubby blond-haired idiot. I'm worried for my sister."

"As a lawman," said Barney, "I think Gladys's concerns are valid. You just told us yourself that he has a home on The Ridge of The Morning Sun, Maeve — the place liquorice grows. He had a tin of liquorice during the meal in Eva's garden, and you told us he enjoyed growing things from seed, and I must say, my honed policing instincts have always told me there was something off about him."

"Hilda warned us of a man with coal black hair," said Willow. "And Derek's hair *is* pretty dark in the portrait we saw of him."

"He has no boat, though," said Maeve. "Derek has never enjoyed water travel, he prefers to travel using magic. As a trusted companion, I have afforded him the ability to do so. Only a select few have the power of transportation. I cannot imagine Derek travelling by boat, he prefers to make a more dramatic entrance."

"That's a small part of the puzzle," said Barney. "Look at the bigger picture."

Maeve's eyes darkened. "And you think Derek was the intruder you found on the boat last night? I don't think so. I would sense his presence had been here, and I sense no remnants of his aura."

"He used powerful magic," said Mum. "He put a forcefield over his boat, it would be easy for a man with that sort of magic to disguise his aura."

Maeve shook her head. "Yet he took nothing from your boat, and did no damage. Maybe it was a coincidence, maybe it was a wizard who wanted to know more about you. I've heard you've caused quite a stir in the city; young people are walking around with their britches around their thighs and making strange music with their mouths. People are talking about you. Maybe the intruder was simply curious to see a boat from the mortal world, and to find out more about who you are."

"Word would have had to have spread fast," I said. "We came back here straight from The Nest of Vipers. News of Barney and Boris's performance couldn't have travelled that quickly."

"Eww!" said Boris, from beneath the dinette table. "Rosie's been sick again, it nearly landed on my hoof, would somebody please put her outside? I'm trying to eat!"

Rosie had been unwell since we'd returned to the boat. We'd put it down to her eating one of the rotten fish which lay in a forgotten wicker basket on the dockside, happy that the rotting flesh would soon leave her system with no ill effects. Rosie was as protected from illness by magic in The Haven as much as the rest of us, but as we'd found out from Granny's happy herb hangover — the protection didn't extend to guarding us from the unpleasant after effects of what we were foolish enough to ingest.

Barney scooped Rosie up in his arm and carried her gently to her basket. He lay the poorly cat down, and placed a blanket over her as Willow knelt beneath the table and scooped up the cat's vomit in a paper towel. She emerged from between our legs with the paper towel close to her nose, her nostrils dangerously close to the yellow mess. "It smells odd," she said, standing up. She sniffed it again and bristled with excitement. "It smells of liquorice!" She hurried to the bin. "And I bet that twig she chewed up this morning smells the same!" She reached into the bin, the sounds of empty tins clanking as she searched for the chewed up remains of the stick we'd pulled splinters of from Rosie's gums. She stood up, holding the mushy mess wrapped in a paper towel. "As I thought," she said, sniffing it. "Liquorice! The man on the boat last night must have dropped it!"

"It's very toxic to cats," said Boris. "She'll be okay soon enough, though."

"Come on, Maeve," said Granny. "I know you don't want to consider it, but you have to! You've seen Derek with liquorice, which is a prized rarity which only grows where he lives, and now we find some on the boat the day after an intruder broke in! Derek must be involved — too many clues point toward him, and my sister is with him! She may soon be the seventh missing witch, and goddess only knows what he intends to do with those poor women! I've always said he has perverted eyes!"

Maeve looked between us. She formed an arch with her fingers and closed her eyes. "I'm still doubtful, but I will transport myself to Derek's home in the East and —"

"The east!" I said. "You told us that the writing on the stone near the castle you found said that the one with the true power would come from the east! It must be him!"

"A jewel was mentioned too!" said Granny, the worry for her sister not preventing her from buttering more bread. "Derek has a jewel on top of that pretentious staff of his! He'd better keep his staff away from Eva, or I'll snap it in two!"

Maeve stood up, urgency etched in her features. "You people must go and search for the depths. With a very heavy heart, I will visit Derek. I'll return when I have answers, and you must summon me should you discover answers. I feel my hold on The Haven weakening, and I fear that whoever has the women captive is planning something terrible."

A swirl of smoke marked Maeve's departure, and the rest of us hurried from the boat, heading to the edge of town where Twiggy had told us we would find the spire of light, and possibly, the depths.

CHAPTER FOURTEEN

a gang of teenage boys, with their underwear
on display, stood at a corner, attempting to
beatbox. When Barney had finished signing auto-
graphs for them, they gave us directions to the spire
of light, which we followed earnestly. The route took
us down narrow alleys and wide roads, until after
almost half an hour of walking, we approached the
edge of the city, the buildings becoming sparser and
with fewer people present.

"I must say," said Boris. "I'm really feeling it
today. I've got a skip in my step and I'm brimming
with energy!"

"It's the magic," said Granny. "You're beginning
to feel it, Boris. You're from a magical family,
remember — I'd hazard a guess that if you didn't

have hooves at the end of your limbs, you'd be able to cast a spell or two."

"Well it feels remarkable," said Boris, sauntering ahead. "Almost like I've been on the brandy all day, but without the anger in my belly or the craving for a kebab."

Long shadows crossed our path as the sun dipped in the sky and evening approached, and soon we neared the stone bridge which spanned a small stream the gang of teenagers had told us to look out for.

"The spire should be on our right," said Barney, checking the map he'd sketched out in his notebook. "Among the trees. In a valley."

Barney led the way, following a well-worn foot-path, the stone smooth from centuries of foot traffic. He craned his neck to see past low hanging tree branches and stepped over a fallen log, warning us to watch our step. The scent of crushed pine needles and earthy wet moss filled my nostrils, and the musical repertoires of song birds was a pleasant change from the harsh squawks of the seagulls which had made the dockside their home, leaving white deposits on the roof of *The Water Witch*, and stealing fish from the fishermen as they landed their catches.

Barney rounded another corner, and an ivy covered stone spire appeared through the trees, narrow at the top, and thickening as it disappeared

AN EYE FOR AN EYE

into the ground, the base overgrown with bushes and thick grasses. Barney stopped. "Someone's coming," he said. "I can hear footsteps."

Three large trolls appeared around a bend in the path and stared at us. Dust clung to their leathery skin and worn out clothes, and they approached us with an air of distrust. "What do you lot want?" said one, his voice tired. "What are you doing here?"

I thought quickly. "We're here for work," I said. "The man with black hair told us to come. He said he had a job for us."

"You're too late," said the biggest troll, his eyes glowing amber. "The works done. It was finished yesterday, we're the last crew out, we did the final clean-up today. It was good pay while it lasted, but it's back to earning pennies working in the quarry for me." He looked at us in turn, a smirk curling his rubbery lips. "Anyway, what work did you expect to do? None of you look strong enough to lift the metal we've been building with."

"We're the interior designers," said Granny, with a bow. "We've come to add the finishing touches."

"It could do with more than some finishing touches," said another of the trolls. "It's a miserable place, whatever it's for. I'm used to being below ground, but that room feels bad."

The third troll wiped his brow, smearing more

dust across his forehead. "Any place with a hidden entrance and a password is bad news," he said. "I'm glad to be out of there, it gave me the chills."

"Hidden entrance?" said Granny. "Where is it?"

"The clue is in the name," said the first troll, "it's hidden, and if you'd been given work here you'd have been told where it was and what the password is. I smell a rat — you're not here to work, are you?"

"We are!" said Granny. "How dare you accuse me of fibbing, and the rat you can smell is the stink from your armpits. I can smell it from here."

"A feisty one," said the tallest troll. "Maybe we should tie them up and wait for the boss to come back, he told us to look out for busybodies."

One of the trolls took a step towards us. "He'll give us extra silver and liquorice," he said. "I vote we tie them up."

"You can try," said Mum. "I'll turn you into toads. You've already got the complexion, I just need to work on your size."

The largest troll laughed. "Magic won't work here," he said. "You're too close to the spire. Only the boss man's magic works here."

"The lead," said Barney. "But surely that would stop his magic working too?"

"The light giving jewel on top of the spire powers his magic," said the smallest troll. "It —" He let out a pained gasp as the biggest troll slapped him on the back.

"Will you stop talking and help me tie them up? We've said too much already."

Granny slipped a hand into her pocket. "If it's money you want, I've got plenty." She tossed the money pouch from hand to hand, making it jingle seductively. "How does three gold pieces each sound — for telling us where the entrance is and giving us the password."

The smallest troll's eyes glinted. "*Three?* Imagine what we could do with sort of money, boys?"

"How about we take *all* their gold and tie them up anyway?" said the nearest troll. "*And* get some silver and liquorice from the boss."

"You could try that," said Granny, "but even without magic, do you think we'd let you tie us up without a fight? The tall ginger man is stronger than he looks, and the goat has got a set of teeth which he'd love to get around your family jewels."

Boris bared his teeth and growled, and Barney flexed a thin bicep.

"I'm tired," said the smallest troll, covering his crotch with shovel sized hands. "I don't want to fight. Let's just take the gold and bugger off, I fancy a beer. We're never going to see the boss man again anyway. He won't know who gave them the password."

The leader relented with a frustrated sigh, which

added an extra three inches to his barrel chest. "Okay," he said, "hand it over."

"Show us the entrance first," said Granny. "I wasn't born yesterday."

The troll bared his teeth in a hideous smile. "I can see that," he said. "You're wrinklier than my family jewels will ever be."

Boris growled again. "Don't you speak to her like that," he warned, saliva dripping from his teeth. "I'm feeling particularly fit today. I'll make short work of ensuring none of you ever father another… troll-let."

"Pups," said the troll. "We call them pups, but I get the picture. There's no need for threats of that magnitude. Come with us, we'll show you the entrance, then we can get out of here for good. I'll be glad to see the back of this place."

The trolls turned around and led us along the last stretch of footpath, taking us into a valley, until we stood in the shadow of the spire. The stone work looked centuries old, and the ivy which shrouded it grew from vines as thick as a man's arm. I craned my neck to look upwards, using a hand to shield my eyes from the low sun. "There's the jewel," I said, pointing at the baseball sized chunk of crystal at the tip of the tower. It glowed dimly, the light hardly visible in the beams of sunlight which poured through the tree canopy.

"You can hardly call it a light," said Willow.

"It glows brighter at night," said a troll. "Especially for the last week. We don't work at nights, but whatever the boss has being doing over the last six nights has made the jewel glow so brightly I can see it from the mountain I live on."

"What's the spire for?" said Mum. "It seems odd, out here on its own."

Barney pushed aside some foliage at the base of the spire. "This isn't all of the spire," he said, scooping some earth aside. "The rest of it is buried."

"That's not all that's buried," said a troll. "The spire is just one part of a whole mansion house, and there's other buildings down there too, lost beneath the ground."

"How do we get in?" said Granny, becoming impatient. "Show us the entrance or you won't be getting your gold."

The tall troll pointed at a large nondescript rock, its surface weather worn and smooth. "It's right there."

"Password?" said Granny, jingling the money pouch.

The troll opened his mouth to speak, but was silenced by his friend, who shook his head. "Whisper it to her," he said. "Let her speak it. Maybe the boss man can tell who opened it — we don't want the blame if these lot cause him problems."

Granny held her nose as the troll placed his lips

next to her ear. "No offence," she said. "But have you heard of mouth hygiene?"

Th troll grunted and whispered a short sentence. Granny looked at him. "It sounds very vengeful," she said.

"The boss seems like a vengeful man," said the troll. He held his hand out. "Gold."

"Not until I've seen it open with my *own* eyes," said Granny, stepping forward and gazing down at the rock. She cleared her throat. "An eye for an eye," she said, her voice loud and deliberate.

The rock trembled a little, the dry soil at its base shaking and a deep groan coming from within it — as if it had a voice. Granny took a step backwards as the rock twisted and turned, its hard form becoming soft and rubbery, until with a gentle hiss it slid to the side, revealing a gaping hole with a set of stone steps leading into the darkness.

"Amazing," said Barney.

"Gold," said a troll. "Now."

"It's a small entrance," said Granny. "How on earth do you get all the lead down there? It must be a real struggle."

"There is a river running below us," said the troll, his hand making a grab for the money pouch, which Granny expertly side stepped. "He brings everything he requires in by boat. The entrance is hidden by a waterfall on the opposite edge of the city, near the mountains."

"How do we close it after us?" I said.

"Repeat the password when you are inside and the entrance will close. Now give us the gold, or you *will* have a fight on your hands. I'm beginning to think your goat is all bleat and no bite."

Granny handed over the coins, carefully counting out three pieces into each troll's hand as they formed a queue before her. "Thank you," she said, as the trolls headed into the trees, leaving us to gaze into the void.

"I'll go first," said Barney. "I can see flickering light at the bottom of the stairs. There must be torches down there."

Cold creeping air rose from the entrance, musty and thick, and I swallowed hard. "It feels wrong," I said. "It feels evil."

"There's dark magic here, no doubt," said Mum. She licked her lips and frowned. "I can taste it."

My skin crawled as a soft voice came from the air behind me, the sound itself brushing the nape of my neck with warmth. I turned to see a shimmering shape, struggling to take form, and surrounded by trails of red smoke, swirling in and out of existence. "Hear me," came the voice again, distant and ethereal, with no real substance.

"Maeve?" I said. "Is that you?"

With everyone's attention on the apparition, it spoke again, distant and haunted. "It is me, Maeve. I cannot take form here, there is dark magic blocking me. I barely found you. The signals from the stones I gave you is weak. As am I. I bring bad news of Eva, Gladys."

"What news?" said Granny, her hand on her chest. "What's happened to her? What's happened to my sister?"

Maeve shimmered and faded, her shape barely visible, as if covered by a veil of muslin. "I went to Derek's home, and Eva is not there. There has been a struggle, and I fear for her safety. Derek's staff was tossed aside, the jewel which decorated it missing, as is he. I fear you were correct, I fear Derek has moved to the darkness. I fear for your safety, and I cannot help you... I cannot reach you."

"A jewel missing from Derek's staff, a jewel on top of the spire, and a jewel mentioned in the inscription near the castle you found, Maeve," said Willow. "What does it mean?"

The air popped and crackled, electric swirling among us, and Maeve briefly took on her solid form, her eyes scared and her voice urgent. "I have no answers, but you are our only hope. All of you. I feel darkness approaching. I fear for The Haven and everyone in it, I sense you are in the presence of great danger, but you must hurry, you must —"

Her words were cut off by an abrupt puff of red smoke, and Maeve was gone, a final shimmering of faint light the only proof she'd been there.

"You heard her," said Granny, rushing for the entrance into the depths. "My sister needs me."

"She needs *us*," I corrected, following her.

CHAPTER FIFTEEN

*B*arney had pushed his way past Granny, refusing to allow her to descend the steps before him, his face set with an urgency I'd never seen before. He was as nervous as the rest of us, and he had every right to be, without any magic of his own — although I'd felt my own magic draining from me with every step nearer to the spire we'd taken. We were unprotected, all of us mortal in a place where powerful and dark magic resided.

Barney led the way down the steps, and I followed him — so close that I could hear his breathing coming in heavy anxious puffs. Boris's hooves clicked on the stone steps behind me, and the narrow corridor darkened as Willow repeated the password Granny had spoken, and the entrance closed with an ominous thud.

We spoke in hushed tones as we descended the long flight of steps, none of us with the magic available to conjure a light, and each of us holding tightly to the clothing of the person in front. Soon Barney spoke, his voice calmer and his breathing less laboured. "I can see the bottom," he said. "There *are* torches."

Barney stepped onto the dusty ground at the base of the steps, and relief flooded me as I stepped behind him. The passage was much wider than the staircase, and the claustrophobia which had been building in me was washed away by the warm light emitted by the flaming torches which lined the walls of the passageway.

Musty air filled my nostrils, bringing to mind the smell of *The Water Witch* when I'd bought her; unloved and damp throughout. A cool breeze blew across my face and the nearest torch flickered. As my eyes adjusted to the darkness, crevices in the walls began to take shape, and as a torch burned bright as another breeze ran past it, the faded letters of a sign high on the wall came into focus. "It's a shop," I said. "A very old shop."

"We're in a buried street," said Boris. "Not a corridor."

Willow wiped her hand across a smooth part of the wall, and the surface below the dirt reflected the torchlight like a mirror. "Glass," she said. "A window."

Barney glanced above his head. "The tree roots are holding the roof up," he said. "I'm surprised these buildings are still standing with all that weight on top of them."

The tree roots *were* the roof. Gnarled and thick, and high above us, the old roots twisted into one another, forming a shelf on which the ground soil lay. Smaller roots hung in clusters like strands of long grey hair, and the occasional drop of water fell to the floor, pooling against the ancient walls of crumbling buildings. It must have taken centuries for nature to form the ceiling, and I wondered when the forgotten street had last seen daylight, or heard the singing of a bird.

"Which way?" said Mum, her head twisting left and right, ignoring Barney's architectural concerns.

"I think we should head towards the spire," I said. "I tried to estimate the distance we travelled along the steps. I'm guessing we're thirty metres below ground level and the staircase was about two hundred metres in length." I pointed to the right. "The house with the spire must be that way."

Granny rushed ahead, taking a torch from an iron bracket on the wall. "Quickly," she said. "Something tells me Eva is here. I can sense her. I always could, even without magic."

Barney handed me a torch and took another for himself. Willow and Mum followed suit, and soon we resembled a mob of angry villagers walking the buried village streets. The only things missing were the pitchforks, and without magic we could have used them. Any weapon would have been better than nothing.

We cast long shadows as we walked, which dragged over the walls of derelict buildings and over the thick trunk of a long-rotted tree which stood in what had once been the front yard of a small cottage. The street widened and the cottages turned into larger houses. Smaller alleyways and streets led off the route we were following, and as we passed a turning to the left, my nose told me of a scent I was familiar with. "I smell the river," I said, "and diesel fumes. Derek must be here, and if he's got Eva, they must have come by boat. We should look."

"So much for Derek using magic to transport himself everywhere," Willow said. "Maeve was wrong about that, wasn't she?"

"He'd have to use a boat," said Mum. "It's possible for him to transport another person with himself, but that person has to be a willing participant in the magic. Eva wouldn't have come without a fight. He'd have had no choice but to bring her by boat. The same as the three witches the dwarfs saw tied up. I'm sure Derek would have liked to have magically transported his victims around The Haven, but no witch would have gone with him willingly."

"Don't use that word," said Granny. "*Victim*. It makes it sound so final, like there's already no hope for those poor people. No hope for my sister."

We headed down the side street, walking toward the smell of river and fuel, the light from my torch showing a very different surface below our feet than the one we'd recently been walking on. "Look," I said. "There's footprints everywhere."

"And gouges out of the ground as if heavy objects were dragged," commented Boris, his nose close to the ground. "It smells of trolls too. This is the route they used to transport the lead and building equipment. I hear running water too; the boat must be nearby."

He was right. The unmistakable sound of a fast running river was close. I took a few more steps and held my torch ahead of me. The red hull of a boat shone back at me, and we hurried toward it, not caring if anybody hostile was aboard the vessel, only caring about the safety of Eva and the other six witches. We reached the river quickly. The bank-side had obviously once been used as a docking point for boats, and rusty mooring posts dotted the stone quay — the red boat tied to one of them with a thick rope, looking out of place among the rotting dereliction of its surroundings. A rat slithered into the water as it heard us approach, its beady eyes reflecting the light of the torches, and its torpedoing body leaving a wake as it swam with the current.

"Only Derek and rats would feel at home down here," said Granny, lifting a leg as she prepared to climb aboard the boat.

Barney stepped in front of her. "No, Gladys," he said. "None of you have magic while we're down here, my police training makes me the only one equipped for this situation."

Granny gave him a smile and stepped aside. "Be careful, Barney," she said, placing a hand on his forearm. "We all love you. You know that, don't you?"

Barney nodded and squeezed Granny's trembling hand. He leapt aboard with a smile in my direction, his long legs making easy work of climbing the hull wall, and his hair a vivid red under the torchlight. Granny was right. We did love him. I loved him, and the seriousness of our situation hit me in the gut with a surprise blow which made me gasp. "Please be careful," I said, as Barney climbed the ladder to the upper deck where the entrance hatch to the hold stood proud.

He nodded and lifted the hatch, the hinges creaking and the boat rocking as dark water sped beneath it. The boat wasn't big, but was large enough to carry the tonne weight of lead the dwarfs had sold Derek each time he had visited them. It was more than large enough to hide somebody in the shadows of the hold, though, but my senses told me the boat would be empty, they told me that we would find our answers below the spire with the jewel. In the long-buried house.

Barney held the torch above the hole, peering into the hold. "It looks empty," he said. "I'll make sure." He lowered himself into the hull, and a thud from inside, followed by muffled footsteps, told me he was safe.

Flame-light flickered on the hull, and a curling shape of gold caught my eye — the sweeping tail of a letter. I'd thought the boat was unnamed, but it was apparent that Derek didn't clean his hull very often. Layers of grime covered the boat's moniker, but with a few vigorous wipes of my sleeve I exposed enough of the painted letters to make sense of them. "*A Vision of Beauty*," I read aloud.

"He didn't name it after himself then," said Granny. "*The Ugly Bastard* would have been more appropriate."

Barney's movement through the boat was easily detectable by the sound of his footsteps, which echoed with an alien presence in the otherwise abandoned world we found ourselves in. Finally, his head emerged from the hatch, and he made his way slowly off the boat and onto the bank. "There's nobody aboard," he said, standing next to Granny, "but I did find this."

Granny's strangled whimper fed into the fear I already felt. The piece of fabric that Barney held was soaked in blood, the floral pattern typical of Aunt Eva's fashion sense, and the discarded chains he held in his other hand, bundled next to his torch, spoke of imprisonment.

"Eva," said Granny.

"There's not much blood in the boat," said Barney. "The fabric was caught on a nail, I think she cut herself as she pulled it free. I'd expect to see a lot more blood if somebody was... well... you know."

"Murdered," said Granny. "Just say what you mean."

"Can witches be murdered?" said Boris, pushing himself against Granny's leg in an attempt to comfort her.

"Of course," said Granny. "Especially down here with no magic, but even *with* magic a witch can be killed. The Haven only protects us from death by natural causes, not death at the hands of a psychopath."

"We should go," said Barney. "We'll follow the footsteps from the boat — I'm certain they'll lead us to the house with the spire."

CHAPTER SIXTEEN

*B*arney was correct, as we'd all suspected he'd be. The footsteps and disturbed earth beneath our feet led us straight to the rusting gates of a large house, the hinges weakened by centuries of neglect, their wrought iron load tilted and twisted. The house loomed at the end of a driveway, our torches illuminating the old walls and roof. The spire we'd known we'd find thrust upward from the centre of the roof, vanishing into the tangle of tree roots which formed a dark, living sky.

"I feel Eva," said Granny, stepping through the gateway. "I know she's here."

The house was large, and dead trees formed a splintered landscape in what would have once been an impressive garden. Barney led the way along the rubble strewn driveway, the light from his torch picking out an old sundial and an ornate birdbath, both of no use in the dark and lifeless underground world.

"A light," said Barney, nearing the entrance, the wooden doors cracked and held open by rotted debris. "I see a light inside and I smell smoke too."

"Look," said Mum, taking a step backwards and lifting her torch.

Smoke drifted from a ruined chimney, torchlight turning it amber as gathered like a cloud amongst the roots, its tendrils spreading through the canopy.

"A fire," I said. "That answers any questions about anybody being at home."

"Maybe the kettle's on too," said Willow, the tremble in her voice betraying her attempt at seeming upbeat.

A floorboard creaked as Barney entered the house, and he glanced at us. "Be careful," he warned. "Stay behind me, all of you."

At the end of a long corridor, lined with stone sculptures and dusty furniture, the wall was painted a flickering orange from the light which poured from an open doorway. The fire. We ignored the sweeping marble staircase which loomed on our left, and followed Barney as he edged closer to the room, reaching down to pick up a length of wood and brandishing it as if it was his police nightstick. I grabbed a rusty length of metal, happy to feel its weight in my hand, and the rummaging scuffles behind me told me everyone else was arming themselves too. What I expected to do with a piece of metal against whatever dark magic Derek possessed, I didn't know, but as I gripped it tighter, its solid reassurance gave me some hope.

The crackle of burning wood grew louder as we approached the doorway, and I jumped in fear as torchlight picked out the haunted eyes of an old man in a portrait which hung on the wall next to me. Barney came to a stop a few feet from the doorway and looked over his shoulder, his eyes serious and his brow furrowed. "Boris," he whispered. "We're the only men here. We should go in first."

"Of course," said Boris, pushing past me and taking his place next to Barney, like a strange breed of horned guard dog.

"Sexist," murmured Granny.

"Really, Granny?" I said. "Now?"

"Nerves," said Granny, squeezing my shoulder. "And I can't help calling it out *wherever* I see it. It's innate."

Boris nudged Barney's leg with a horn. "After you, copper," he said.

Barney gave me one last smile, and with Boris at his heels, stepped into the room. He was silent for a few moments, and then appeared again, his face less concerned. "It's empty," he said. "Come on."

The room smelt of burning logs, damp furniture, and soil. The large fireplace roared with a bright fire, and a pile of fresh logs stood next to the hearth. A chair and a table, both wiped clean, had been dragged in front of the fireplace — the only sign that somebody had benefited from the fire's warmth. The other furniture was as decrepit as the rest of the underground world. Dust covered everything, and wood had rotted while metal had rusted. Pictures still hung on the walls, their subjects lost beneath grime, some of them hanging at odd angles — ready to crash to the bare floorboards at any moment.

"He's been here," said Granny, gazing around. "Derek's been here, with my sister, and those other poor witches. I can sense him. I can sense evil."

Willow stood before a canvas on the wall, wiping the dirt from the oil paint with her fingers. "I thought so," she said, rubbing at some stubborn grime with a thumb. "I could make out a little of the painting under the dirt, look, its a boat. A red boat."

The paint was badly faded beneath the dirt. A large circular window sat high in the wall opposite the picture, and I suspected it had once allowed streaming sunlight into the room which had ruined the painting, instead of the roots which now searched and poked for a route through the broken glass and rotting frame.

"Who is it with the boat?" I said, leaning closer to

the canvas, my nose almost brushing the old artwork. "Derek?"

The shape of a person next to the boat was hard to make out, and the paint had cracked where the face should have been. It was a man though, I was sure. Or maybe a woman.

"I don't know," said Willow, "but it's definitely the same red boat that Barney's just been on. I can tell by the shape."

"This place is really old," said Barney. "That painting is really old. How can it possibly be the same boat? It would have rotted by now."

"Magic," said Granny. "Come on, Barney, use that noggin of yours."

"I see something shiny," said Boris, peering beneath an old chair in a dark corner. "In the dust." He reached beneath the chair, using a hoof to drag the object towards him, dust rising into the air in billowing clouds which made him cough and splutter. "It's a piece of cloth," he said. "With little jewels on it."

The oval piece of cloth almost crumbled as I picked it up from the dust at Boris's feet, and two tiny jewels fell from their mountings. It took a few seconds to realise what it was I was holding, the two holes through which string or elastic could be threaded finally making it apparent. "It's an eye-patch," I said. "Covered in tiny jewels."

Footsteps thudded at the doorway, and Mum gave a frightened gasp as a figure shrouded by shadows walked into the room. "I wondered where that had got to! I lost it almost five hundred years ago, and to think it was under that chair all the time! Oh well, it matters not. I think the one I wear now is much nicer!"

"Hilda?" said Granny. "Is that you?"

The figure stepped into the light cast by the fire, and the bejewelled eye-patch she wore glinted in the orange light. Granny was right, it was Hilda. "Hello, Gladys," she said. "How nice of you to bring your family for a visit. I think we'll have a wonderful night together. I've been looking forward to today for a long time, a very long time indeed."

"What's going on?" said Granny. "Is Eva here?" And Derek?"

Hilda smiled. "Yes, Gladys, they're both here. I'm sure they'd love to see you. They're waiting patiently for you in my new room — the room that those dumb trolls built for me. I like to call it my burn room, but you might like to call it the death room, or the room of agonising pain, because that's what you're going to experience in there."

Mum lifted her hand, but no sparks danced at her fingertips. "What are you talking about, Hilda? What's happening here?" she said.

Hilda laughed, her whole body shaking. She

looked at Willow, a smile on her lips. "You've cleaned my painting for me," she said. "How kind. That's me with *A Vision of Beauty.* A lovely name for a seer's boat, don't you think?"

Barney lifted the piece of wood in his hand, and I closed my grip on the length of metal I carried.

"You're not thinking of attacking a helpless old lady, are you?" said Hilda, her face twisting with anger. "I've got no time for fighting with you people. I think it's about time I took you all to my burn room, it's dark outside and tonight the jewel on my spire is going to glow brighter than it's ever glowed before."

Granny took a step towards Hilda, but one step was all she manged. Hilda lifted both hands and magic crackled at her fingertips. Sparks of red and blue danced in the air weaving between us, brushing my skin with a cold evil which made me shudder. Granny sank to her knees as if being pushed to the floor by a heavy weight, and Barney's spine arched as he was flung against a wall, his torch dropping to his feet where the flame was extinguished by a shower of Hilda's sparks, and the length of wood he'd armed himself with turning to dust.

"Impossible," groaned Granny. "How do you have magic and we don't?"

Hilda laughed again, her magic disarming and immobilising us all, the flames in the hearth growing brighter, lighting the room and warming the air. "I'll tell you everything when I get you all into my burn room," she said. "And I won't leave a thing out. My plan has taken centuries to bring to fruition and I'm dying to tell you all about it. I've had to bite my tongue for so many years, but tonight I can finally tell my tale! Tonight, I can shine as bright as the jewel on top of my spire!"

Torches fell from people's hands, and the metal rod I carried dropped to the floor, clunking as it hit the wooden boards. I tried to move, but invisible tethers of magic held me still, icy cold against my flesh, becoming tighter each time I struggled against them.

"This is such fun!" laughed Hilda. She waved her hand, green sparks flowing from her fingertips, swirling through the room and searching for targets. Willow gasped as sparks flooded her nostrils, and Boris grunted as his ears were invaded. A stream of green approached my face, the dancing lights forcing their way into my mouth, warming my throat and making me gag.

"A spell of total control," said Hilda. "You're all under my command. Now follow me, all of you, in silence. Eva and Derek are waiting for you, and Maeve will be along soon. It's going to be a good night!"

Hilda walked from the room and like obedient servants we followed her, taking one forced step after another, helpless against the powerful magic which controlled us, and unable to speak.

"This way," said Hilda, walking ahead of us in the darkness, only her voice leading the way. "My burn room is where the ball-room once was; right beneath my spire. You're going to love it, I'm sure!"

CHAPTER SEVENTEEN

*H*ilda led us through the darkness, magic fizzing around us in brightly coloured sparks which occasionally lit up a sculpture or painting as we were led along corridors. Finally, Hilda ordered us to stop. A tall wooden door loomed before us, its brass knobs dusty and faded with time. "I had some memorable times in here," said Hilda, pushing open the door which groaned in protest, "but tonight's going to the best of them all."

Bright light burst from the open doorway, and my eyes stung as they adjusted to their new surroundings. We followed Hilda into a huge room, the walls, ceiling, and floors lined with sheets of dull silver metal. Lead. Lots of it, covering every surface, creating a room that was void of character, but full of dread. In the centre of the room, hanging from the metal sheet ceiling on a length of copper coloured wire, was the source of the bright light which flooded the room. A glass ball, the size of a melon, emitted a white light and tiny sparks of blue electric, which cut through the air like lighting, making a sizzling sound as they arced from the ball.

Below the sphere was a large round stone plinth on which was stacked a layered pile of wood, with a tall wooden stake protruding from the centre, the top of which stopped a few inches shy of the glowing ball. It was built in an identical manner to the pyre in the painting in Maeve's library, and icy tendrils of dread gripped my heart as I imagined what Hilda intended to do.

Next to the pyre stood Derek and Eva, both immobilised by the same magic that Hilda had used on us, only their eyes free to move.

"Join Derek and Eva," Hilda commanded. "Make a semi-circle around the pyre. I need you all to be able to see. The burning will begin when everyone's in place and the guest of honour arrives."

Unable to prevent my feet from moving, I shuffled into position, taking my place next to the pyre, with Boris on my left and Barney on my right. I used every available grain of inner strength I possessed, reaching inside myself for something that would help me break the magic which controlled me. Spells from Granny's book flashed before me, but I could do nothing to make one work, it was as if my body wasn't mine, as if I was peering out of the eyes of another person, unable to do anything to control my fate or the fates of the people I loved.

Panic surged through me in a powerful wave that made me nauseous, and I made eye contact with my sister, desperate to connect with somebody, desperate for somebody to tell me it was all going to work out fine, but Willow's eyes reflected my own fear, her pupils large and tears welling. I couldn't swivel my eyes far enough to the right to see Barney, but his rapid breathing told me he was scared too, and why wouldn't he have been? It was obvious that Hilda meant somebody great harm, and it was as equally obvious that she intended to make the rest of us watch the horror. Boris was a blur of white in my peripheral vision, but I managed to roll my eyes far enough to the left to tell he was staring at Granny, whose eyes were calm as she attempted to convey the same emotion to anybody who looked at her — trying her best to keep her family soothed.

Hilda stood to the side of the pyre, her bony hands held before her thin body and her eyes dancing with excitement. "I think it's time for the guest of honour to make an appearance," she said. Her hand moved across her body as she cast a spell, and the air next to her shimmered and hissed as Maeve slowly took form, her face lined with anxiety and her hands bound with a silvery thread. "What magic is this?" she said. "Hilda, what are you doing?"

Hilda looked at Maeve. "Am I to take your voice too, like I have the voices of everyone else present at this ceremony? Or will you remain calm? Listening to what I have to tell you?"

"I will remain calm," said Maeve, her eyes searching the room, trying to make sense of what was happening, looking for a way to escape. "Why are we here, Hilda? How am I here, and why do I have no magic, yet you so obviously do?"

It filled me with revulsion, and hatred for Hilda — knowing that we were going to be forced to watch Maeve burn. She'd been named the guest of honour, and I doubted that the moniker had been bestowed upon her for any less heinous reason. It seemed that for the second time in her long life, Maeve was to be burned alive, and we were to be the witnesses. Bile rose in my throat, and the acrid flavour of guilt filled my mouth, as I found myself hoping that should Maeve not be the only victim of Hilda's madness, I wished death upon Derek and not somebody I loved.

Hilda gave Maeve a long drawn out smile, the corners of her mouth curling with hatred as she prepared to speak. "You have no magic, Maeve, because I choose it to be that way. Anything that happens in this room is of my making. I control you, all of you, and soon I will control your haven. In fact, my power is spreading as we speak, for the last six nights I've been feeding the jewel on top of my spire with magic, and as the jewel fed on its prey, my power has been spreading throughout this land, weakening you, and making it easy to transport you here against your will. Soon I will be the ruler of this dimension, and I fear I shall not rule it with such a ..." Maeve made a growl of revulsion as Hilda took her hand and ran a finger over the soft skin. "... fair hand as you have," she finished.

Maeve's eyes dimmed, and her jaw muscles rolled as she clenched her teeth. "Six nights... six missing witches," she said. "What have you done, Hilda? What have you done to those poor women?"

Hilda's laugh echoed around the room, bouncing off the walls and ceiling, the lead dulling the high-pitched mirth. "They burned well," she said. "Their magic left them just as I predicted it would, deflected by the lead walls and targeted at my orb, feeding my jewel and spreading my power across the land. You see, you're not the only witch who releases a burst of magic when she slowly burns to death. It would appear that the pain causes all witches to do so. Call those six deaths practice runs if you will, I'm appreciative that they gave their lives — although they didn't go easily — but tonight is the main event, tonight is the night that I recreate the day you burned, Maeve — all those years ago, *and* recreate the stream of power which created this land. The power will be harnessed to me through my jewel, and then I shall finally enter the castle which you thought you had hidden so well. The castle that belongs to the one true ruler of The Haven. The castle which belongs to me."

"You would burn six witches so you could rule The Haven?" said Maeve. "If it must be that I am the seventh as it seems is to be my fate, then I will go without a struggle, but you must promise not to harm any of these other people. If you do not promise me that, then I shall fight my death with every ounce of power I have within me. I will do everything to make my magic work against you as I burn, everything in my power to foil your plan."

"How very brave," said Hilda, her voice low. "How very, very brave of you, Maeve, but I'm afraid that tonight is not your night. You shan't be tethered to my stake with flames melting the flesh from your bones, screaming as the heat boils your blood, and choking as the hot clogging smoke fills your lungs. No, that won't be you, Maeve, you are just here to watch — to know you are beaten, after all these centuries." She lifted a hand and extended a finger. She pointed at us, one by one, turning in a slow spin, her eyes glinting as they met mine, but passing me quickly, moving on to the next person. "No, tonight, I will be burning …" She stopped spinning and jabbed her finger at the intended victim. "Gladys Weaver!"

Granny's eyes dropped briefly, but quickly lifted in defiance and met Hilda's. As Granny winked at the woman who was to murder her, my gut twisted and my heart struggled to beat. Only the dark magic which held me in place prevented me from collapsing.

———

HILDA WAVED a hand in Granny's face, showering her with red sparks of magic. "You have your voice back, Gladys, and soon you will have your magic back, but not for long."

"You vile old bitch," said Granny. "I've never trusted you."

"Why are you doing this, Hilda?" said Maeve. "I thought we were your friends."

"The time has come," said Hilda, scraping a long fingernail over Maeve's cheek. "Finally. The moment I've been waiting for. The moment I've ran through my mind over and over again. I've often fantasised about how you were going to react when you realised who I really was, when you realised that you never escaped me, when you realised that you were beaten." Maeve shuddered as Hilda licked her face, her tongue sliding over Maeve's chin and across her lips. She drew her tongue back into her mouth and gave a satisfied sigh. "And now that moment is here, it tastes so much better than I ever thought it would. I taste fear on your flesh, I taste uncertainty, and I taste curiosity. You want to know why sweet little Hilda the seer has burned six witches and is about to burn another."

Maeve nodded, her eyes searching Hilda's face for answers. "I do."

Hilda took her eye-patch between two ragged fingernails and lifted it slowly, moving her face closer to Maeve's, her tongue flicking like a snake's, and her breathing ragged and excited. "Do you recognise me, Maeve? Do you remember my eyes? Do they scare you? One of green and one of brown — a gift from god, a gift given to me so I could search out your type and burn them where I found them!"

"It can't be," said Maeve. "*You* can't be!"

"But it is, and I am," said Hilda. "I am the Witch-finder General, although that title is redundant in this land of yours — finding witches is not hard, and I no longer wish to burn all of your type — ruling them would give me far more satisfaction, and if the truth be known, I've become quite fond of The Haven and *some* of its inhabitants. I'm hoping Gladys Weaver will be the last witch I am forced to burn, because to be quite honest, the smell of burning flesh is very hard to get out of the nostrils."

I strained at the magic that held me, but could do

nothing. A sickening pressure built within me, and I knew that if Maeve didn't possess the power to save Granny from the flames, then nobody did.

"Show yourself," said Granny. "If you are the Witch-finder."

Hilda laughed, the sound perverse and haunting, tinged with an evil which made Granny's eyes darken. Hilda's whole body shook violently, as if she were a marionette at the end of strings controlled by a psychopath. The air around her moved and whispered, vibrating in time with the pulses of energy which shook her. She lifted her face towards the ceiling, the old flesh on her chin shifting on the bone, as if being twisted into a new shape by an invisible hand. Gold and red sparks danced around her, and her voice deepened as she laughed louder, the very clothes on her thin frame changing as her shoulders widened and she grew in height. The skin on her hands crawled, and her long feminine fingernails shortened, like a cat drawing in its claws, until they were short and at the tips of thick masculine fingers.

"No," said Maeve.

"How?" said Granny.

In place of Hilda, a man stood before us, over six feet in height, a tall black hat on his head and a high necked white shirt beneath his dark clothing. He gazed around the room, his eyes, one green and one brown, studying us in turn. He lifted his hat in a macabre greeting, revealing long dark hair, and he split his mouth in a manic grin. "I *am* the Witch-finder General!" he shouted. "And tonight, I will burn one more witch!" He took a deep breath and looked around the room he'd built, pride evident in his expression. "First, though. Let me tell you all a story —"

"I don't want to listen to your stories," said Granny. "If you're going to kill me, get it over with. I don't want to hear one more word from your hateful mouth."

The Witch-finder bent at the waist, and put his face close to Granny's. "I would advise you do listen, Gladys Weaver. It will make you understand why you should concentrate on burning well when I wrap you in flames, it will help you understand that if you struggle or fight my magic, that I will kill the remainder of your family, one by one, until I get the result I desire." He cast his eyes over the rest of his captives. "If anything, listening to me will buy your family some more time in your presence before they lose you for ever. It looks as if they love you very much, which will aid me immensely when you burn — you see, love is a vital ingredient which was missing from the last six burnings. Look, Gladys, look at the love they have for you — they all have tears in their eyes. Even that annoying goat is weeping."

Granny closed her eyes, not in defiance, but to hide the tears I'd seen glimmering in the bright light. She opened them again and started directly at the man she'd known as Hilda for so many years. "Tell your story if you must, Witch-finder," she spat.

CHAPTER EIGHTEEN

*L*ike a motivational speaker on a stage, the Witch-finder clasped his hands behind his back and began pacing, the heels of his black leather boots clicking on the lead floor. "Where should I begin?" he pondered.

With a sigh, he lowered himself into a seating position on the stone plinth, using the logs piled high behind him as a backrest. "I know!" he said, raising a single finger. "I'll start at the beginning — as the old saying goes. I'd offer you all a seat, but I enjoy watching you standing, trapped by my magic. It makes me realise how powerful I've become."

"Nobody's as powerful as they think they are," said Maeve.

The Witch-finder smiled, a glint in his eyes. "So very true," he said, "and how very pertinent to the story I have to tell. You see, Maeve, you didn't conjure The Haven into existence because you were more powerful than any other witch. It was purely a matter of luck that I chose to build the fire I burned you on in the place I did."

"In the middle of my village," said Maeve. "With the people I loved being forced to watch me suffer."

"Indeed," said the Witch-finder. "In fact, this house is built in the exact spot your pyre was built on. In a different dimension of course, but on the exact spot. The spire is built directly where the centre of the fire would have been."

Maeve's demeanour had become calmer and relaxed, but I could tell by the fierce spark in her eyes that she was struggling against the powerful magic which swirled through the room. I hoped with every fibre of my being that she would find the strength within her to save Granny from the awful fate she'd been threatened with.

The Witch-finder gazed upwards, as if drawing on memories, his face serene — the complete antithesis of the panic which gripped me, clawing at my gut and quickening my heartbeat, forcing my breath from me in frightened gasps.

Granny looked at me, the message in her eyes one of calm, but with a hint of hope. I took comfort from her, concentrating on trying to access my magic — if

Granny could muster hope in such a situation, then so should I.

The Witch-finder gave a low laugh and continued with his story, his words wrapped in a pride that forced me to focus on my hatred for him, willing myself to find my magic. "I found you easily, Maeve," he said. "When you turned that man into a toad for a day, as punishment for stealing eggs from you, some of the villagers couldn't wait to report you for being a witch. When the news got to me I came quickly, I hadn't burned a witch for almost a full month, and I was itching to smell roasting flesh again."

"Evil," said Granny. "That's what you are."

"On the contrary," said the Witch-finder. "I was on the side of good. God gave me a gift — the gift of seeing. My visions began when I was six-years-old, and my mother said it was my special eyes which made my skill possible. I'd already seen Maeve in a vision, but the tell-tale villagers made the job of finding her easier, and saved me a little time."

The orb above the pyre crackled and dimmed briefly, and the Witch-finder looked at Granny. "I am running out of time, as are you, Gladys. The jewel requires more magic." He stood up and began pacing again. "I will tell my story quickly, so as I can get on with the important business of burning you."

Granny laughed, a bitter outburst of defiance. "Do what you must," she said.

"As Maeve burned," said the Witch-finder, "surrounded by people who loved her, and the people who had betrayed her, I heard a strange noise… a throbbing hum the like of which I'd never heard before, and the ground vibrated beneath my feet. As the flames grew hotter and Maeve screamed louder, the sound grew in volume too, until Maeve vanished in a flash of light." He closed a fist. "One moment she was there and the next… she was gone. The villagers thought it had been God's doing of course, but I knew different. I'd seen a flash of light at the base of the fire, and heard the humming sound grow louder. I knew it was magic, but I also knew it hadn't all been of Maeve's doing — she'd been in too much pain to cast a spell that powerful. Of that, I was certain."

"I watched you smiling as I burned," said Maeve. "The anger I felt for you fuelled my magic."

"Oh, your magic had a part in in it all," said the Witch-finder. "But you had help. When the fire had cooled, I searched the ashes. I searched them for a day and a night, finally digging beneath the hardened ground, looking for the cause of the sound I'd heard." The Witch-finder looked upwards. "And what I found sits on top of my spire, where it has done for six hundred years, waiting for this day."

"The jewel," said Granny.

The Witch-finder nodded. "Indeed, the jewel. Luckily for me, I had another witch captive in the horse-drawn cage I travelled with — what I now know was an oriental witch, a beautiful prize I wished to give to the king. She was too important to burn — a witch from a foreign land had never been seen before. The king would have rewarded me handsomely."

"Did you make her suffer too?" spat Granny. "You vile creature."

"I would have, of course," said the Witch-finder. "But it wasn't to be. I required her help, and I promised to slaughter every man, woman, and child in the village if she refused to comply. The cage bars were made of lead — I knew, even all those years ago, that lead was a deterrent to magic, so I took a risk by releasing her, but she valued the lives of inno-cents above her own. She gave me the help I needed."

"How does *your* magic work in this lead lined room?" said Maeve. "I do not understand."

"My jewel is more powerful than any magic you have ever known," said the Witch-finder. "The orb above the pyre is connected to it, and only I am able to access it. The magic flowing from my jewel cannot be hindered by lead, for it is the very jewel that created The Haven, and I am joined with it as one. The lead prevents you weaker witches from accessing magic, and try as hard as you might, that fact will not change – you are powerless in this room, and you will be powerless against me outside this room when my jewel has been fully powered by magic."

"I don't —"

The Witch-finder interrupted Maeve with a wave of his hand. "No more time wasting. I must hurry." He sat down again and continued. "The oriental witch told me what the jewel was — a simple diamond which had reacted to Maeve's magic, amplifying its power and causing an opening to another dimension. This dimension. The dimension you call your own, Maeve. As you know, though — as is inscribed on the stone near the castle — the person with the one true power will rule The Haven."

"It mentions a jewel too…" said Maeve, her voice faltering, realisation spreading across her features.

The Witch-finder laughed. "Now you see — my power *and* my jewel!" He glanced to the side. "Now, where was I? Oh, yes! The oriental witch used magic to work out what had happened. She knew a dimension had been opened, and she knew that if I passed into that dimension carrying the jewel which had formed it, I would possess the very heart of the dimension, and when you possess the heart, you control the rest of the body. I would become magical, and rule this land."

"So why don't you rule The Haven?" said Granny. "You've been here for a long time. A very long time."

"She betrayed me," said the Witch-finder, dark anger lining his face. "As I passed into The Haven, through a portal she'd opened, she cast a spell and chipped a piece of diamond from the stone I carried. She kept that piece of diamond, and though it was only small, it dramatically reduced the power of the stone. The stone has provided me with magic in this land, but has never been powerful enough to afford me total control over The Haven..." The Witch-finder's tongue stroked his top lip, and he smiled. "... Until today."

He reached into his pocket and withdrew a jewel. He held it between finger and thumb, and inspected it, rolling it from left to right, the light from the orb reflecting off it, the sharp corners sparkling.

He placed it on the stone plinth next to him and straightened his collar. "When I arrived here, in The Haven, only a few days after Maeve, I already had magic, but I knew I wasn't as powerful as I could have been. I needed a disguise — without strong magic I knew I'd be no match for Maeve, and it was highly doubtful that Maeve would have afforded the man who burnt her any mercy, so I used the power of the stone to shift my shape into the opposite of what I'd been. Instead of the handsome young man you see sitting before you today, I took on the shape of a grizzled old woman. The only problem was my eyes. I could only control their colour temporarily, for minutes at a time, so I came up with the idea of an eyepatch. It fitted my new persona perfectly, and as I still had my gift of visions, I became Hilda, the seer. It was perfect, and worked a treat, and what fun I had lifting my eyepatch occasionally, taunting Maeve when I was in her presence, but knowing the colour of my eyes could shift at any moment. The risk gave me such a wonderful feeling of excitement!"

"All the time we spent together," said Maeve. "To think that you fooled me for centuries makes me sick."

"Oh," said The Witch-finder. "Don't be too hard on yourself. I did begin to enjoy myself here, and I valued people's friendship too. When I first arrived in The Haven, I built this house, placing my jewel at the highest point, spreading its power, trying to take control of the land. As other witches fled the justice of the mortal world and found their way to The Haven, more people built homes near mine until there was a village.

I became popular in the village, using my gift of seeing to help people. After a century, I almost forgot who I really was, and when this village was hidden by a landslide, I moved to the east and began a new life, befriending people like yourselves and spending my time enjoying my boat and growing herbs, spices, and the best liquorice in The Haven. I enjoyed my life, and *nearly* forgot about my desire to control The

Haven, until I had a powerful vision, almost fifty years ago, and now that vision is about to come true." He stood up, and took Granny's hand in his. "It's almost time for you to burn, Gladys."

"So, it was you all along," said Granny. "You were the dark haired man the dwarfs spoke of, and you were the man on Penny's boat."

"Of course," said the Witch-finder. "And my visit to the boat was very important for helping today's events go smoothly, Gladys."

"Why?" said Granny. "You didn't take anything."

"Oh, I did," said the Witch-finder. "You see, when we all sat together in Eva's garden, eating her mediocre food, I'd already burned four of the six witches — one a night, but I simply couldn't get enough magic into my jewel to make my plan work. Those witches just weren't powerful enough. When I saw you, surrounded by your family, I realised something of great importance. I realised that when I'd burnt Maeve, she'd been watched by people who loved her.

Love is a very potent magic, as you know, and I understood that as you were the eldest and frailest of your family, the love for you would be immense. As your family watch you burn, their love for you will enhance your magic and help power my jewel. As for what I took from your granddaughter's boat — well, to make sure your magic is deflected off the lead walls and collected in the orb above the pyre, there needs to be some of your essence inside it. I made a potion from the hair of each of the other six witches, and I thought it prudent to do the same for you."

"My hairbrush," said Granny. "I knew I'd packed it."

The Witch-finder nodded. "Indeed, and the potion helped draw you here, guiding you to clues and leading you too your demise."

The Witch-finder looked to his left, an eyebrow raised. "Derek is gesticulating wildly with his eyes, perhaps he wishes to speak." He flicked a hand, releasing sparks. "Speak, Derek, but make it quick. When my jewel brings down the spell surrounding the castle of the one true ruler, and I take residence, then you'll have plenty of time for an audience with me, but for now, make your words count."

"Burn me!" said Derek. "I'm powerful. Don't burn Gladys. Not in front of her family. It's barbaric!"

I tried to twist my eyes in their sockets, but couldn't swivel them far enough to see him. Derek was willing to sacrifice himself to save my grand-mother, and I couldn't even look at his face.

"Oh, Derek," said Granny. "I misjudged you. I'm sorry."

"It's a brave gesture," said the Witch-finder. "But there's not enough love in the room for you, Derek. Your magic just won't work."

"I'm sorry, Gladys," said Derek, "for anything I ever did to upset you."

"You just be good to my sister when you all get out of here," said Granny. She looked at the Witch-finder. "They will all get out of here, won't they?"

Granny's eyes darkened as the Witch-finder cupped her frail chin in his hand. "I give you my word that if you go to your death willingly, and the magic works, then I will harm no one. I won't need to, I will control this world. If you struggle, though, and my magic fails. I will burn your family one by one until the magic *does* work."

Granny nodded. Her fate accepted.

"Wait!" said Derek. "Why did you take the jewel from my staff?"

The Witch-finder scowled. "I know you're wasting time, trying to preserve the life of Gladys for as long as possible, but I *will* answer your question. The vision I spoke of having fifty years ago was unclear. It showed me that I needed to burn witches, and it showed me that I needed to come back to my buried home and build this room of lead beneath it. The vision showed me the spell protecting the castle being broken, but it did not show me everything. Do you remember my vision at Eva's home, Derek?"

"I do," said Derek. "You spoke of a great power, and you spoke of a man with hair as black as coal."

Hilda had also spoken about a blossoming

romance, and I shed a tear as I thought of Granny's love for Charleston. She would go to her death having never told the man she loved how she felt.

"That was foolish of me," said the Witch-finder. "I didn't mean to speak so candidly. I was excited you see, and when I become excited I speak my visions freely. I saw a vision of myself in this room, and I saw great power, I couldn't help myself, the words escaped my mouth. They did no harm though. My plan is working as expected. Nobody suspected me."

"What were you excited about?" said Derek. "What made you speak so freely?"

The Witch-finder picked up the small jewel from the stone plinth. "I was excited about the jewel in your staff, Derek. I had another vision as we sat at that table, one I kept to myself. I saw that the owner of the piece of diamond the oriental woman stole from me, was in that garden. Nobody else had a jewel like yours, Derek. The jewel that was set in the top of your staff *had* to be the missing piece, and when I place it beneath the fire Gladys will die in, I will have recreated Maeve's burning perfectly — the love for her, the pain, *and* the jewel beneath the blaze."

"But that jewel —"

The Witch-finder silenced Derek with a wave of his hand. "You too, Maeve," he said, taking her voice too. "The only sounds I wish to hear are the anguished screams of Gladys Weaver as she melts."

"You'll never be forgiven," said Granny. "You know that, don't you?"

"I neither expect or wish to be," said the Witch-finder. "I need no forgiveness. I will be immortal i this land, and I will rule this land. I care not for the forgiveness of any of my subjects.

He reached inside Granny's dress, eliciting a shout from her. "Burn me to death all you like, but never touch me without my authority!"

"I'm not trying to violate you, Gladys. I'm looking for the dementia cure which Maeve gave you. I need your magic working correctly while you burn, otherwise I may as well be burning a mortal. You won't be able to use your magic in this room, but with dementia still afflicting you, your magic will never leave your body, however hot I make the flames."

"It's on a chain, around my neck," said Granny. Realisation dawned in her eyes, and she stared at the floor to the left of me. "Charleston," she said. "When I take this cure, you'll be released from the body of Boris. The spell that trapped you in the goat was cast in the mortal world, the lead in this room won't stop it from being reversed. You must tell my son that I love him, and tell him never to come here —"

"Silence!" said the Witch-finder, taking the cork from the small glass vial which contained the cure.

Granny ignored him. "And, Charleston — I want you to know that I lov—"

The Witch-finder silenced Granny with magic, and her eyes dimmed, all hope leaving them. She stared ahead of herself, blankness on her face, as the Witch-finder forced the vial between my grandmother's lips and poured the contents down her throat.

A crackling sound next to me and a rush of warm air on my legs told me that the spell trapping Charleston in Boris's body had been reversed. Charleston would wake in Granny's guest bedroom, knowing what was happening in The Haven, unable to help us, and aware that he would probably never see any of us again.

Desperation fuelled more tears, and I wished I could move an arm to wipe them from my cheeks. I wanted to appear brave. I wanted to *be* brave, but the only sensations that coursed throughout my body were those elicited by fear.

The Witch-finder took Granny's hand in his. "Look," he said, glancing to my left. "It's a simple goat again. Perhaps I'll keep it as a pet, it can keep my lawns trimmed when I move into my castle."

Tears ran freely down Granny's cheeks, and she did as she was told when the Witch-finder gave her what would likely be the last instruction she would ever follow. "Get onto the plinth, Gladys. Your pyre awaits, as does your martyrdom."

CHAPTER NINETEEN

*M*y whole body ached as I fought the spell which held me captive. The panic and perseverance in Willow's eyes showed she was doing the same. I didn't need to be able to see everybody to know they would be fighting too, even Barney, whose heavy breaths grew louder as Granny climbed onto the plinth and took her place on the pyre.

With Granny's back against the stake, and her legs knee deep in wood, the Witch-finder waved a hand. The spell forced Granny's hands behind her back, and she gave a grimace of pain as her hands were tied to the pole with a strand of silvery magic.

The Witch-finder gazed at his victim, a sickening pride in his smile, and a casualness in the way he spoke which made me shudder. "Have your voice back, Gladys. I'll need to hear your screams."

Granny looked at us in turn. "Don't mourn me in sadness," she said. "And don't remember me as I am now — helpless and tied to a stake, remember me as I was for all the years you knew me before this moment, because as horrible as this moment is — it's only one of the millions of beautiful moments I've lived through with all of you. I give my life freely to ensure none of you will be harmed."

"Yes, yes, very nice," said the Witch-finder. "Very sentimental." He bent at the waist and slipped the jewel he'd stolen from Derek's staff beneath the pile of wood. He muttered something under his breath, and flames appeared at his fingertips. "Now, if you've finished saying your goodbyes, I think it's time we got going. This fire is not going to light itself."

"Willow, Penny," said Granny, speaking quickly. "A woman couldn't have asked for kinder, nicer grandchildren. I love you both, deeply. You've both brought immeasurably joy to my life.

Barney, look after Penny — you're a fine man. I know you'll do good by Penny, and I hope you tell your children that their great grandmother loves them, wherever she is.

Eva, I was wrong about Derek, cherish him and cherish yourself. I love you.

Maggie, my second born, take care of yourself, my dear, dear daughter. You were always there for me, and I appreciate you more than you will ever know.

Maeve, thank you for everything, and I trust you will eventually beat The Witch-finder and rule The Haven again."

Flames flew from the Witch-finder's fingertips, and the hope I'd been holding onto that somehow one of us would be able to save Granny, evaporated in a surge of wretched despair.

The flames took hold quickly, wood crackling as it burnt, the smoke being drawn into the orb above the pyre.

Every muscle in my body fought at the magical bonds which held me, my emotions becoming a tangled mix of anger, fear and desperation. Time seemed to slow in my mind, but the flames that worked their way closer to Granny's legs did not. As the first lick of heat touched her papery skin, she let out a whimper — the sound a cold blade of hopelessness which pierced my heart.

Memories of Granny flooded my mind as flames wrapped her legs in heat, her whimpers becoming loud shouts as she gave way to inevitable panic. I remembered her showing me and Willow how to make cup-cakes, the three of us laughing as we gave

Granddad the single cake we'd flavoured with salt instead of sugar.

I remembered her teaching me how to read, using magic to bring the pictures in the book alive, and never getting frustrated when I couldn't pronounce difficult words. I remembered a beautiful woman, a kind woman, a complicated woman, but a woman I loved. A woman I loved deeply.

Heat spread from the fire, warming my neck and hurting my skin even at the distance I was from the flames, and I tried not to think of the temperatures Granny was experiencing.

As the flames licked at Granny's neck, and her screams mingled with the manic laughter of the Witch-finder, a surge of white light blinded me momentarily, and I had what was only my second vision since I'd discovered I possessed the power of seeing.

It seemed that the lead in the room prevented me from using magic, but it couldn't stop a vision — and even as I watched Granny's face disappear in flames, her screams becoming less intense and her magic visibly pouring into the orb above her head — I became calm, knowing that everything was going to be okay, but not knowing how or why.

The Witch-finder's cackling mirth grew louder as the orb above the fire grew brighter, and Granny became silent, her body hidden by flames, and her magical essence leaving her in beautiful strands of gold and amber which rose from the flames and filled the orb.

My vision faded, but I'd seen all I needed to see – Granny alive, and happier than I'd ever seen her — and I was certain that it was to happen in the *very* immediate future — as certain as I was that the Witch-finder was going to live out his immortality in misery, and not ruling The Haven as he had envisioned.

Willow's eyes had deadened, and I wished I could tell her everything would be okay, but she stared at the flames, lost in her despair.

A loud grating of metal was the first sign that something was not right with the Witch-finder's plan. The sound reverberated through the room, the floor trembling beneath my feet, and a heavy pounding making the walls shake violently.

The orb above the fire flickered, and the bright white light changed — slowly at first, whites becoming blues, then purples, until it throbbed with an angry red which cast the room in a scarlet glow.

The Witch-finder stepped backwards, his face lit with the dancing oranges of the flames, but concern replacing the glee which had emanated from him as Granny had suffered.

"What is this?" he shouted. He looked at Maeve. "Is this your doing, witch?"

Maeve's eyes remained expressionless, and the Witch-finder span on the spot as one of the lead walls groaned, it's surface bubbling and melting as if a great heat was forming behind it, forcing its way through the metal.

Molten lead dripped in a waterfall of silver, pooling on the floor at the base of the wall, and the dim glow of a light beyond the wall became visible, becoming brighter as lead spat and bubbled in its path.

"What is this?" shouted the Witch-finder, stepping backwards. "Who dares do this?"

White light filtered into the room, piercing the scarlet light cast by the orb, and parting the lead wall like the petals of a flower, spreading the metal until a perfect circle was formed. Brilliant blue light filled the hole, a dark shape appearing in the centre, its form becoming clearer as it approached, until it became apparent what it was — the silhouette of a person.

"Who are you?" shouted the Witch-finder. "Tell me!"

The silhouette stopped moving, and a loud vibrating voice filled the room — distant and warped by magic, but unmistakable as to whom it belonged. "Gladys, I'm here, and I love you too!" it boomed. "I have since the day I met you."

CHARLESTON HUANG STEPPED into the room, a closed fist held before him, blue light pouring from the ring on his finger.

"Everything's going to be okay," he said, confidence oozing from him. "I promise."

Light poured from his ring in a powerful stream which wrapped itself around the Witch-finder and thrust him upwards, pinning him against the ceiling, where he remained, silent and unmoving.

Charleston turned his attention to the fire, guiding a stream of light into the flames. The crackling of burning wood gave way to a melodious humming which changed in pitch and tempo as the flames rose and fell, becoming a dancing kaleidoscope of colours, the oranges and reds mixing with pinks, blues, and yellows, until there were only flames of white and blue.

The heat from the flames gave way to a gentle breeze which cooled my face, and I gazed into the fire, screaming inwardly as I caught a glimpse of Granny's charred lifeless face.

Charleston stood next to the fire, his dark eyebrows narrowing as he concentrated, the light from his ring flowing into the cold blue flames.

Granny's face was hidden once more, and the flames grew taller, beginning to spin, twisting and turning, moving closer to the stake in the centre of the fire, until they wrapped Granny's body in light, enveloping her in a shimmering beauty which I instinctively knew was good magic. A healing magic.

"It's okay," murmured Charleston, his body rigid. "You're okay, Gladys."

Flames transformed into beams of twisting light, which shattered the orb above the fire and spread throughout the room in a sudden rush of power which filled me with a sense of good – a sense of love.

"Nearly there," said Charleston, the light from his ring brightening as my magical bonds weakened.

I collapsed to the ground with a gasp as the Witch-finder's magic finally failed, and struggled to my feet, rushing towards the pyre. "Granny!" I shouted.

Barney joined me, dragging me into his arms, his hand on my head. "Penny," he sobbed. "I tried to get free. I tried so hard. I couldn't move."

"I know," I said, my tears wetting his shirt.

Willow and Mum hugged, and Boris the goat bleated in panic, galloping in circles around the room until Charleston waved a hand, sending sparks cascading over the animal's back, calming it.

"Granny!" I shouted again, knowing she would be okay, but needing to see her – the urgent desire twisting my gut and closing my throat as I sobbed.

Charleston's ring glowed brighter, throbbing on

his finger, and the stream of light pouring from it stopped abruptly. The blue light surrounding Granny began to fade, and her face became clear, her skin complete again, and her eyes bright. Her voice came softly at first, her words incomprehensible, but as the light slid down her legs and across the burnt wood, evaporating into the ether, she cleared her throat and smiled. "Hello everybody," she said. "That was a bit of a palaver, wasn't it?" She looked at Charleston. "Oh, you're here. I was under duress when I said what I did. Ignore me, it was the ramblings of a silly old lady about to meet her maker."

Charleston reached up, easily plucking Granny from the pyre and placing her at his feet. He drew her close and planted a soft kiss on her blue hair. "Don't worry, Gladys. I've wanted to hear those words come from your mouth for a long time. I love you too."

Granny's shoulders shook, and the sound of her gentle sobs were muffled by Charleston's chest as he pulled her close.

Charleston gazed around at the rest of us. "Are you all okay?" he asked.

When he was happy we were unharmed, he looked at Maeve. "I have the power to transport you all out of here," he said. "The spell guarding the castle has fallen, I can sense it. I will send you all there, where you can wait for me. Gladys needs to recover, and I'm sure you would all like to get out of this terrible place. Will you look after them until I get there?"

"Of course," said Maeve. "It would be my pleasure... Charleston Huang."

"Where are you going, Charleston?" I said.

Charleston looked at the ceiling, from where the Witch-finder gazed down at us, his eyes glazed, and his body rigid. "I'm not going anywhere. I'm going to deal with him once and for all. I'll be along as soon as I'm done. I'm sure you'll all have questions for me."

"I'll stay with you," I said.

Charleston shook his head. "No, you should —"

"I want to," I said.

"If Penny's staying, I'm staying," said Barney.

Charleston nodded. "Okay," he said. He waved a hand, and red smoke enveloped everybody else, including Boris. With a shimmering of air and a loud popping sound, they vanished.

I looked up. "What are you going to do with him?" I said.

"You're not going to kill him, I hope," said Barney. "I know I don't hold jurisdiction here, but the death sentence seems wrong."

"I'm not going to kill anybody," said Charleston. "Even though he's responsible for the death of six witches here, and only he knows how many in the mortal world." Charleston gazed around the room. "I have a fate far worse than death in mind for him. I only wish we could have saved those six women, but he burned them to ash, there's nothing I can do. Gladys was lucky I got here when I did, with her heart intact I was able to regenerate the rest of her body, any longer and it would have been all over for her. Maybe then I'd have been considering the death sentence, as hypocritical as that sounds."

"It's not hypocrisy," said Barney, smiling at me. "That's love."

Charleston waved a hand, and the Witch-finder fell from the ceiling, sprawling at our feet, groaning in pain. "He'll never know love," said Charleston.

The Witch-finder gazed up at us, the eyes he was once so proud of, now dull and scared. "What will you do with me?" he said.

Charleston looked around the room and with a flick of his fingers cast a spell which closed the hole he'd made to enter the room. "This room will be your prison," he said. "For two hundred years. Then I will reconsider."

"No," said The Witch-finder. "Kill me."

Charleston shook his head. "No, and I'll cast a spell preventing you from harming yourself, and removing your need for sustenance. You'll live here, in the dark, with no requirement for food or drink. You're going to pay for what you did, Witch-finder."

"No! You can't do that to me," begged the Witch-finder. "I'll go insane being alone for that long. It's crueller than death!"

Charleston smiled. "Oh, you won't be alone, not all of the time." He gazed into a corner, and made a gentle beckoning motion with his hand, as if calling a frightened animal. He lowered his voice, and spoke softly and slowly. "Make yourselves shown. Your suffering is over, you can walk among us now."

Nothing happened for a few moments, but suddenly the air burst into life with tiny orbs of light. Zipping left and right like a swarm of bees, they joined with one another, forming larger and larger orbs, until the transparent shapes of six women took form.

"What are they?" I said, knowing the answer, but not believing it could be true.

"Ghosts," said Barney.

"Yes," said Charleston. "Ghosts walk in this world, and the mortal world. They rarely make themselves seen, but in this case, I think they'll enjoy the exception. They are free to leave this room as they wish, but I'm sure they'll spend a lot of time with their murderer."

"No!" said the Witch-finder. "Kill me, I beg of you!"

The six ghosts approached us, pushing cold air in front of them, and hovering a few inches from the ground. They smiled at us, their silvery bodies undamaged by flames, and their clothes intact.

One of them came closer, cold air swirling past us as she moved. "Thank you," she said, her papery voice out of sync with her lips, arriving a second after her mouth had moved. "Thank you for searching for us, it was not to be that you would find us in time, but we appreciate you trying, and we thank you for allowing us to take our revenge. You should leave now, we don't wish to frighten you."

"I wish you well," said Charleston, "and I'm sorry we couldn't save you."

"No!" screamed the Witch-finder, pushing himself along the lead floor, his boots sliding as they searched for purchase. "Please! Not this!"

Red smoke clouded my view as Charleston prepared to transport us from the room, but I could still make out one of the ghosts rushing from the corner, a scream pouring from her mouth, deafening in the metal lined room.

She approached the Witch-finder and her face transformed. Flesh hung from her bones, and as Charleston cast the spell my nostrils filled with the sickly aroma of burning flesh, and the blood curdling scream of the Witch-finder followed us for a few seconds after we'd left his self-constructed prison.

Charleston's spell set us down at *The Water Witch*,

and I rushed on-board, scooping Rosie from the bow decking and holding her close to my chest.

"I thought we'd pick up your boat on the way." said Charleston. "Maeve said something about a lake at the castle — I'll have us there in a jiffy. I don't know about you two, but after all the excitement, I could kill for a brandy and a nice fat cigar!"

CHAPTER TWENTY

*C*harleston had transported us to the perfect spot on the lake, landing *The Water Witch* with hardly a ripple on the glass smooth surface to show the boat had appeared from thin air, and was not sailed into position.

Grassy banks filled with mature trees and teeming with wildflowers made a beautiful mooring, and after securing the boat, the three of us made our way up a steep pathway leading to the castle.

The huge building held a commanding position above the lake, its many turrets and towers reminding me of the fairy tales I'd read as a child. I'd not have been surprised to see a knight in shining armour appear around a corner, or spot a damsel in distress in one of the highest windows.

Boris the goat had been put out to pasture in the

main courtyard. He had a whole lawn to himself and a trough full of fresh water which he lapped from as Charleston approached him. "I'm sorry if I filled you with Brandy and cigar smoke," Charleston said, kneeling next to the animal's head, "but Gladys assured me you were protected by magic, you'll suffer no ill effects."

Boris nudged Charleston's hand with his snout and gave a gentle bleat.

"I don't think he cares," said Barney.

"It'll be strange speaking to you, as… you, Charleston," I said. "It'll take some getting used to."

"Call me Charlie," he said. "And treat me how you treated me when I was a goat. I enjoyed it, it's been the best time of my life."

"Look," said Barney, pointing skyward. "Up there."

"Coooeee!" shouted Granny, leaning between the turrets of a high tower. "We're up here, King Charleston, and we've conjured up a feast fit for a king… and his queen! There's brandy too, and some beautiful cigars!"

Charleston laughed. "We'd better get up there," he said. "*Queen* Gladys demands our attention."

Long spiral staircases and narrow corridors led us through huge halls and past open terraces, until we finally found the high balcony the feast was waiting for us on.

Derek and Eva sat together, giggling as they sipped glass goblets of red wine, and Willow and Mum picked at the food on the long wooden table, Willow opting for grapes and cheese, and Mum choosing hunks of roast beef which she slathered with mustard.

Maeve stood up as we made an entrance, her smile as bright as the sun and her hair blowing in the breeze. "Here's the hero of The Haven!" she said, clapping. "Charleston Huang!"

Mum, Willow, Derek and Eva joined in the applause, but Granny rolled her eyes. "Don't be so daft," she said, flopping into the large wooden chair at the head of the table. "It'll go to his head! Stop that clapping, a brandy is all he'll want!"

"Granny!" I said. "Two hours ago, you were dead — burnt to a crisp on a fire. Charleston saved you — he brought you back to life, of course he's a hero!"

Granny poured brandy into a glass. "I didn't say he wasn't, I *said* it would go to his head." She lifted the glass and thrust it towards Charleston. "Here you go," she said. "Get your laughing gear around that, and then you can tell us all how the heck you passed from one dimension to another, through a metal wall, and brought a dead woman back to life... then you can have a cigar."

CHARLESTON SIPPED HIS BRANDY. "I felt different since I arrived in The Haven," he said. "I felt stronger every day — more healthy, you know?"

Granny patted his hand. "I know, dear," she said. "It was the magic in the air."

Charleston nodded. "And as we approached the spire of light I brimmed with energy — I realise now it was the magic from the jewel on the spire, but I just thought it was the fresh air. When we got underground though, the feeling passed. I felt like a normal... goat again."

"The lead," said Maeve.

Charleston sipped his drink. "Yes, the lead."

"Then how on earth did that ring of yours manage to slice a hole in the lead?" said Granny. She looked around the table. "They've filled me in on what happened while I was... on fire, and then dead. It sounds like you made quite the entrance."

"The moment that vial containing the cure touched your lips, Gladys," said Charleston. "I was back in my body. In your guest room. I thought I'd gone blind at first, but I remembered you'd put a light shade on my head to help me blend in. When I'd removed that, I knew something had changed within me." He looked at his hand. "The diamond in my ring was glowing and vibrating, and I knew everything — I mean I could *see* everything — the history of the diamond in my ring, and what I had to do with it —

how I could use it to save you all and deal with the Witch-finder."

"How?" sad Maeve. "Tell us."

Charleston looked out across the scenery. The lake, far below us, sparkled in the sun, and the balcony we were gathered on, built on one of the castle's highest towers, gave us a view as far as the horizon. "It began with my ancestor," he said. "The oriental witch the Witch-finder spoke of."

"Of course," said Willow.

Charleston smiled. "When she cast the spell, which chipped the diamond in my ring from the stone the Witch-finder carried into The Haven, her magic tangled with the magic of the Witch-finder, and she stole a vision from him, one which was meant for the Witch-finder, but one he never saw. Luckily for us, or today may have ended very differently."

"A vision of what happened in that lead room?" said Mum.

Charleston nodded. "And everything that came before it. My ancestor was not a seer, and that was the only vision she ever had. She did what the vision told her to do. She entered The Haven, travelled to the west, and conjured this castle into existence. Using the stone to cast the spell which guarded it, and ensuring that only the stone could break the spell. A key if you will."

"And she wrote the inscription on the stone," I

guessed. "And when she wrote the one true ruler would come from the east, she meant the far east in the mortal world!"

"Exactly," said Charleston. "From China, to be precise. When the castle was built, she left The Haven, knowing the stone must never again travel to this land until the day it was needed... today. She saw that a man would bear the ring, and would only come when needed, and I'm the first boy in the Huang bloodline. Every generation of witch the stone was passed down to was told they must never bring it here, and they must only visit The Haven on occasion, never arousing the suspicion of The Witch-finder. They knew he was here, and they knew he was in disguise, but not *what* disguise. He could have been anyone — they needed to stay away — they couldn't risk the Witch-finder finding them out."

"So they sacrificed their immortality in The Haven to die in the mortal world and keep the stone safe," said Granny. "No wonder none of your ancestors are here Charleston. They all gave their lives knowing that one day you would need the stone to save The Haven from the Witch-finder."

Charleston nodded. "Indeed, and they couldn't tell anyone, not even Maeve, because the vision *had* to come to fruition. They couldn't risk changing the future. Of course, I didn't know I was a witch until the day *you* told me. My grandmother had decided to take the secret to the grave — giving up on the vision for reasons known only to her, but fate brought us together, Gladys, as you said it had, and it seems that fate had a very good reason for doing so."

Willow, Granny, and I had found out that Charleston came from a magical family when we'd discovered a photograph of his grandmother.

Granny had recognised her as a witch she'd once known, and told Boris that she'd chosen to die outside The Haven -- although Granny had wrongly surmised the reason she'd given up her immortality was that Charleston's grandmother was ashamed of her witch heritage.

Charleston's grandmother had never informed her own daughter that she was a witch, and without being able to practice and develop her magic, Charleston's mother would have remained ignorant of the fact that she had magical powers.

Charleston had never known he came from a magical background, until Granny had told him, and I was beginning to believe Granny was correct when she had blamed fate for bringing Charleston into her life – fate had made sure that the vision had come true and The Haven had been saved.

"Your grandmother was trying to save you," I said. "She knew the vision said a man would bear the stone, and you were the first boy to be born in the bloodline. She didn't know if you would die saving

The Haven or not, so she chose to keep you safe by ending the vision with her death. Her love for you came before her promise to ensure the vision came true."

"And the safety of the people in The Haven," murmured Charleston. "I don't know what to think of her actions."

"But why didn't she destroy the stone?" said Willow. "With the stone still in the family, it was possible the vision would always come true, were she told anyone else or not."

"A guilty conscience," said Charleston. "When I was eighteen, I received a parcel from a lawyer containing the diamond and a letter from my grandmother. The letter said that she hoped I would know what to do with the stone one day. I had it mounted in a ring and never really thought about it again until today. I think the letter was her way of telling me, *without* telling me."

"It all sounds a little sexist to me," said Granny.

"What's sexist about it?" I said. "Did that fire scramble your brains?"

Granny wriggled her fingers in my direction, and smiled. "Careful with the insults. I've got my magic back, remember!" She reclined in the large wooden chair. "I'll tell you why it's sexist. Charleston's family refused to bring the diamond to The Haven for centuries, even choosing to die in the mortal world so the stone wouldn't get into the wrong hands. Waiting for a *male* witch to be born, who would eventually save The Haven? *That's* sexism if ever I've seen it."

"The vision told them it would be a boy," said Willow. "I'm not sure visions can be sexist."

Granny smiled. "Everything can be sexist, my dear." She stood up, and clapped. "Now, who's up for some exploring. If I'm to be the queen of this castle, I think I should get to know it a little better, and work out how many servants I'll require."

"You're not a queen, Gladys," said Charleston, "and I'm not a king. There'll be no servants. As far as I'm concerned, The Haven is still Maeve's, and if she wants this castle, she may have it."

"I'll hear of no such thing," said Maeve. "You deserve this castle, Charleston Huang, and you deserve to live here as a kept woman, Gladys Weaver."

"Careful, Maeve," said Barney. "Gladys is a feminist, remember? She doesn't want to be kept by a man." He smiled at Granny. "Your lectures have paid off," he said. "I think I understand feminism!"

"No, Barney," said Granny, with a frustrated sigh. "That only applies to men like accountants, plumbers, or garbage collectors. A feminist wouldn't be kept by a man like *that*, of course not, but when a king takes you as his queen, you throw your principles out of the window and embrace your sugar daddy."

"I'm not a king," said Charleston. "And you're not a queen."

"Lord and Lady?" said granny.

Charleston smiled, the lines around his mouth tightening and his eyes twinkling. "Okay. Lady Weaver it is."

"Really," said Granny. "You land a catch like me and you don't put a ring on it? It's Lady Huang, or nothing!"

"Are you proposing?" said Charleston. "Or are you expecting me to get on one knee?"

"You can forget all about that romance stuff with me! I don't go in for it all that nonsense, but if you want to see my hammer and sickle, my finger had better have a band on it."

"Granny, enough!" said Willow. "Nobody wants to see your tattoo."

Granny winked at Charleston. "I'm game for marriage if you are?"

Charleston took her hand in his and kissed it gently. "Of course I'm game for it," he said. "I love you, Gladys Weaver."

Eva stood up. "I love a bit of... romance — if that's what you can call it — as much as the next person, but I'm tired. It was nighttime in Hilda's sunken village, but it's turning to dusk here a few hours later, I think I'm suffering from what mortals call…"

"Jet-lag," said Derek. "We're in a different timezone."

"Bedtime it is," said Granny. "At a conservative estimate, I'd say that this castle has sixty-four bedrooms, so take your pick."

"I'm sleeping on the boat," I said.

"Me too," said Willow. "I want to snuggle up with Rosie."

"Me too?" said Barney.

"Of course," I said. "You can cook us breakfast in the morning."

" I want a room with a four poster bed, please," said Mum. "And an en-suite."

———————

WITH THE CASTLE a silhouette against the starry sky, on the hill above us, Willow, Barney, and I sat on the roof of the boat, sipping wine and listening to music. Rosie sat next to us, swatting moths, and purring whenever one of us gave her any attention.

Willow gave in to fatigue first, giving a loud yawn and stretching her arms towards the moon. "That's it," she said. "I'm going to bed. I've had enough excitement to last me a lifetime."

Barney and I followed her off the roof, and said goodnight as she closed her bedroom door with another loud yawn. Barney began transforming the dinette furniture into a bed for himself, but I held my bedroom door open. "Come on," I said. "I watched my grandmother die and get resurrected today. I don't want to sleep alone."

With Barney's legs bent at the knees, he managed to fit on the mattress next to me, and with my arm across his chest and my head on his shoulder, the last sound I heard was a distant owl, before I drifted off to sleep quickly, feeling calmer and safer than I had in a long time.

THE NEXT MORNING, after breakfast, Willow, Mum, Barney, and I stood on The Water Witch, waving at the shore.

Granny and Charleston stood side by side waving back at us, with Boris squeezed between them, eating a mouthful of grass.

Derek, Eva, and Maeve had already left, and Charleston and Granny had insisted we had breakfast in the great hall with them, dining on croissants, fruits and berries, and pancakes with wild honey.

Maeve had willingly handed over control of The Haven to Charleston, telling him she'd never seen magic so powerful as the magic he now possessed, and as she'd said, six-hundred years was a long time in the same job. She fancied a change.

Charleston and Granny were making changes. They were staying in The Haven, living in *Huang Towers*, as Granny had named it overnight — and sleeping in separate bedrooms until such time Charleston had made an honest woman of her. Granny had told us that it would be prudent to go hat shopping in the next few weeks, as she wasn't going to be wasting any time.

I steered the Water Witch towards a bridge which spanned one of the four rivers leading off the lake, and with a final wave and shouted promise to Granny and Charleston that we'd be back soon, I opened a portal and gave the engine some power, aiming the bow at the centre of the glowing gold light, looking forward to getting back to Wickford, and happy I was surrounded by people I loved.

The End

ABOUT THE AUTHOR

Sam Short loves witches, goats, and narrowboats. He
really enjoys writing fiction that makes him laugh —
in the hope it will make others laugh too!
You can find him at;
www.samshortauthor.com
email - sam@samshortauthor.com
Facebook - www.facebook.com/samshortauthor/

26825376R00146

Printed in Great Britain
by Amazon